P9-AGT-255

An eternity passed before
Andrew spoke

"Were you afraid I was going to demand a reward, Florence Nightingale?"

Jo Marie's heart went still. "You do remember." They'd spent a single, golden moment together so many months ago. Not once since Kelly had introduced Andrew as her fiancé had he given her the slightest inkling that he remembered.

"Did you imagine I could forget?" he asked quietly. "I went back to that hospital every day for a month," he continued in a deep, troubled voice. "I thought you were a nurse."

The color ebbed from Jo Marie's face, leaving it pale. She'd looked for him, too. In all the months since the Mardi Gras, she'd never stopped looking. Although she'd never known his name, she had included him in her thoughts every day since their meeting. He was her dream man, the stranger who had shared those enchanted moments of magic with her.

Dear Reader,

Although our culture is always changing, the desire to love and be loved is a constant in every woman's heart. Silhouette Romances reflect that desire, sweeping you away with books that will make you laugh and cry, poignant stories that will move you time and time again.

This year we're featuring Romances with a playful twist. Remember those fun-loving heroines who always manage to get themselves into tricky predicaments? You'll enjoy reading about their escapades in Silhouette Romances by Brittany Young, Debbie Macomber, Annette Broadrick and Rita Rainville.

We're also publishing Romances by many of your all-time favorites such as Ginna Gray, Dixie Browning, Laurie Paige and Joan Hohl. Your overwhelming reaction to these authors has served as a touchstone for us, and we're pleased to bring you more books with Silhouette's distinctive medley of charm, wit and—above all—*romance*. I hope you enjoy this book, and the many stories to come.

Sincerely,

Rosalind Noonan
Senior Editor
SILHOUETTE BOOKS

DEBBIE MACOMBER
Christmas Masquerade

Published by Silhouette Books New York
America's Publisher of Contemporary Romance

For Tara
A woman of grace, charm and sensitivity
Thank you

SILHOUETTE BOOKS
300 E. 42nd St., New York, N.Y. 10017

Copyright © 1985 by Debbie Macomber

Distributed by Pocket Books

All rights reserved, including the right to reproduce
this book or portions thereof in any form whatsoever.
For information address Silhouette Books,
300 E. 42nd St., New York, N.Y. 10017

ISBN: 0-373-08405-6

First Silhouette Books printing December 1985

10 9 8 7 6 5 4 3 2 1

All the characters in this book are fictitious. Any
resemblance to actual persons, living or dead, is purely
coincidental.

SILHOUETTE, SILHOUETTE ROMANCE and colophon are
registered trademarks of the publisher.

America's Publisher of Contemporary Romance

Printed in the U.S.A.

Books by Debbie Macomber

Silhouette Special Edition

Starlight #128
Borrowed Dreams #241

Silhouette Romance

That Wintery Feeling #316
Promise Me Forever #341
Adam's Image #349
The Trouble with Caasi #379
A Friend or Two #392
Christmas Masquerade #405

DEBBIE MACOMBER

has become one of Silhouette's most prolific authors. As a wife and mother of four, she not only manages to keep her family happy, but also keeps her publisher and readers happy with each book she writes.

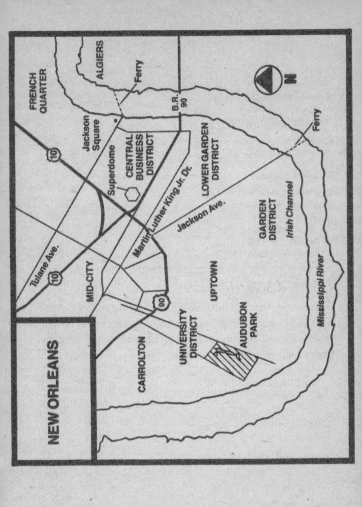

Prologue

The blast of a jazz saxophone that pierced the night was immediately followed by the jubilant sounds of a dixieland band. A shrieking whistle reverberated through the confusion. Singing, dancing, hooting and laughter surrounded Jo Marie Early as she painstakingly made her way down Tulane Avenue. Attracted by the parade, she'd arrived just in time to watch the flambeaux carriers light a golden arc of bouncing flames from one side of the street to the other. Now she was trapped in the milling mass of humanity when she had every intention of going in the opposite direction. The heavy Mardi Gras crowds hampered her progress to a slow crawl. The observation of the "Fat Tuesday" had commenced two weeks earlier with a series of parades and festive balls. Tonight the celebrating culminated in a frenzy of singing, lively dancing and masqueraders who roamed the brilliant streets.

New Orleans went crazy at this time of year, throwing a city-wide party that attracted a million guests. After twenty-three years, Jo Marie thought she would be accustomed to the maniacal behavior in the city she loved. But how could she criticize when she was a participant herself? Tonight, if she ever made it out of this crowd, she was attending a private party dressed as Florence Nightingale. Not her most original costume idea, but the best she could do on such short notice. Just this morning she'd been in a snowstorm in Minnesota and had arrived back this afternoon to hear the news that her roommate, Kelly Beaumont, was in the hospital for a tonsillectomy. Concerned, Joe Marie had quickly donned one of Kelly's nurse's uniforms so she could go directly to the party after visiting Kelly in the hospital.

With a sigh of abject frustration, Jo Marie realized she was being pushed in the direction opposite the hospital.

"Please, let me through," she called, struggling against the swift current of the merrymaking crowd.

"Which way?" a gravelly, male voice asked in her ear. "Do you want to go this way?" He pointed away from the crowd.

"Yes...please."

The voice turned out to be one of three young men who cleared a path for Jo Marie and helped her onto a side street.

Laughing, she turned to find all three were dressed as cavaliers of old. They bowed in gentlemanly fashion, tucking their arms at their waists and sweeping their plumed hats before them.

"The Three Musketeers at your disposal, fair lady."

"Your rescue is most welcome, kind sirs," Jo Marie shouted to be heard above the sound of the boisterous celebration.

"Your destination?"

Rather than try to be heard, Jo Marie pointed toward the hospital.

"Then allow us to escort you," the second offered gallantly.

Jo Marie wasn't sure she should trust three young men wearing red tights. But after all, it was Mardi Gras and the tale was sure to cause Kelly to smile. And that was something her roommate hadn't been doing much of lately.

The three young men formed a protective circle around Jo Marie and led the way down a less crowded side street, weaving in and out of the throng when necessary.

Glancing above to the cast iron balcony railing that marked the outer limits of the French Quarter, Jo Marie realized her heroes were heading for the heart of the partying, apparently more interested in capturing her for themselves than in delivering her to the hospital. "We're headed the wrong way," she shouted.

"This is a short cut," the tallest of the trio explained humorously. "We know of several people this way in need of nursing."

Unwilling to be trapped in their game, Jo Marie broke away from her gallant cavaliers and walked as quickly as her starched white uniform would allow. Dark tendrils of her hair escaped the carefully coiled chignon and framed her small face. Her fingers pushed them aside, uncaring for the moment.

Heavy footsteps behind her assured Jo Marie that the Three Musketeers weren't giving up on her so easily. Increasing her pace, she ran across the street and was within a half block of the hospital parking lot when she collided full speed into a solid object.

Stunned, it took Jo Marie a minute to recover and recognize that whatever she'd hit was warm and lean. Jo Marie raised startled brown eyes to meet the intense gray eyes of the most striking man she had ever seen. His hands reached for her shoulder to steady her.

"Are you hurt?" he asked in a deep voice that was low and resonant, oddly sensuous.

Jo Marie shook her head. "Are you?" There was some quality so mesmerizing about this man that she couldn't move her eyes. Although she was self-consciously staring, Jo Marie was powerless to break eye contact. He wasn't tall—under six feet so that she had only to tip her head back slightly to meet his look. Nor dark. His hair was brown, but a shade no deeper than her own soft chestnut curls. And he wasn't handsome. Not in the urbane sense. Although his look and his clothes spoke of wealth and breeding, Jo Marie knew intuitively that this man worked, played and loved hard. His brow was creased in what looked like a permanent frown and his mouth was a fraction too full.

Not tall, not dark, not handsome, but the embodiment of every fantasy Jo Marie had ever dreamed.

Neither of them moved for a long, drawn-out moment. Jo Marie felt as if she'd turned to stone. All those silly, schoolgirl dreams she'd shelved in the back of her mind as products of a whimsical imagination stood before her. He was the swashbuckling pirate to her captured maiden, Rhett Butler to her Scarlett O'Hara, Heathcliff to her Catherine....

"Are you hurt?" He broke into her thoughts. Eyes as gray as a winter sea narrowed with concern.

"No." She assured him with a shake of her head and forced her attention over her shoulder. Her three gallant heroes had discovered another female attraction and had directed their attention elsewhere, no longer interested in following her.

His hands continued to hold her shoulder. "You're a nurse?" he asked softly.

"Florence Nightingale," she corrected with a soft smile.

His finger was under her chin. Lifting her eyes, she saw his softly quizzical gaze. "Have we met?"

"No." It was on the tip of her tongue to tell him that yes they had met once, a long time ago in her romantic daydreams. But he'd probably laugh. Who wouldn't? Jo Marie wasn't a star-struck teenager, but a woman who had long since abandoned the practice of reading fairy tales.

His eyes were intent as they roamed her face, memorizing every detail, seeking something he couldn't define. He seemed as caught up in this moment as she.

"You remind me of a painting I once saw," he said, then blinked, apparently surprised that he'd spoken out loud.

"No one's ever done my portrait," Jo Marie murmured, frozen into immobility by the breathless bewilderment that lingered between them.

His eyes skidded past her briefly to rest on the fun-seeking Musketeers. "You were running from them?"

The spellbinding moment continued.

"Yes."

"Then I rescued you."

Jo Marie confirmed his statement as a large group of merrymakers crossed the street toward them. But she barely noticed. What captured her attention was the way in which this dream man was studying her.

"Every hero deserves a reward," he said.

Jo Marie watched him with uncertainty. "What do you mean?"

"This." The bright light of the streetlamp dimmed as he lowered his head, blocking out the golden rays. His warm mouth settled over hers, holding her prisoner, kissing her with a hunger as deep as the sea.

In the dark recesses of her mind, Jo Marie realized she should pull away. A man she didn't know was kissing her deeply, passionately. And the sensations he aroused were far beyond anything she'd ever felt. A dream that had become reality.

Singing voices surrounded her and before she could recognize the source the kiss was abruptly broken.

The Three Musketeers and a long line of others were doing a gay rendition of the rumba. Before she could protest, before she was even aware of what was happening, Jo Marie was grabbed from behind by the waist and forced to join in the rambunctious song and dance.

Her dark eyes sought the dream man only to discover that he was frantically searching the crowd for her, pushing people aside. Desperately, Jo Marie fought to break free, but couldn't. She called out, but to no avail, her voice drowned out by the song of the others. The long line of singing pranksters turned the corner, forcing Jo Marie to go with them. Her last sight of the dream man was of him pushing his way through the crowd to find her, but by then it was too late. She, too, had lost him.

Chapter One

Y ou've got that look in your eye again," pixie-faced Kelly Beaumont complained. "I swear every time you pick me up at the hospital something strange comes over you."

Jo Marie forced a smile, but her soft mouth trembled with the effort. "You're imagining things."

Kelly's narrowed look denied that, but she said nothing.

If Jo Marie had felt like being honest, she would have recognized the truth of what her friend was saying. Every visit to the hospital produced a deluge of memories. In the months that had passed, she was certain that the meeting with the dream man had blossomed and grown out of proportion in her memory. Every word, every action had been relived a thousand times until her mind had memorized the smallest detail, down to the musky, spicy scent of him. Jo Marie had never told anyone about that night of the Mardi Gras. A couple of times she'd wanted to confide in Kelly, but the words wouldn't come. Late in the evenings after she'd prepared for bed, it was the dream man's face that drifted into her consciousness as she fell asleep. Jo Marie couldn't understand why this man who had invaded her life so briefly would have such an overwhelming effect. And yet those few minutes had lingered all these months. Maybe in every woman's life there was a man who was meant to fulfill her dreams. And, in that brief five-minute interlude during Mardi Gras, Jo Marie had found hers.

"...Thanksgiving's tomorrow and Christmas is just around the corner." Kelly interrupted Jo Marie's thoughts. The blaring horn of an irritated motorist caused them both to grimace. Whenever possible, they preferred taking the bus, but both wanted an early start on the holiday weekend.

"Where has the year gone?" Jo Marie commented absently. She was paying close attention to the heavy traffic as she merged with the late evening flow that led Interstate 10 through the downtown district. The freeway would deliver them to the two-bedroom apartment they shared.

"I saw Mark today," Kelly said casually.

Something about the way Kelly spoke caused Jo Marie to turn her head. "Oh." It wasn't unnatural that her brother, a resident doctor at Tulane, would run into Kelly. After all, they both worked in the same hospital. "Did World War Three break out?" Jo Marie had never known any two people who could find more things to argue about. After three years, she'd given up trying to figure out why Mark and Kelly couldn't get along. Saying that they rubbed each other the wrong way seemed too trite an explanation. Antagonistic behavior wasn't characteristic of either of them. Kelly was a dedicated nurse and Mark a struggling resident doctor. But when the two were together, the lightning arced between them like a turbulent electrical storm. At one time Jo Marie had thought Kelly and Mark might be interested in each other. But after months of constant bickering she was forced to believe that the only thing between them was her overactive imagination.

"What did Mark have to say?"

Pointedly, Kelly turned her head away and stared out the window. "Oh, the usual."

The low, forced cheerfulness in her roommate's voice didn't fool Jo Marie. Where Kelly was concerned, Mark was merciless. He didn't mean to be cruel or insulting, but he loved to tease Kelly about her family's wealth. Not that money or position was that important to Kelly. "You mean he was kidding you about playing at being a nurse again." That was Mark's favorite crack.

One delicate shoulder jerked in response. "Sometimes I think he must hate me," she whispered, pretending a keen interest in the view outside the car window.

The soft catch in Kelly's voice brought Jo Marie's attention from the freeway to her friend. "Don't mind Mark. He doesn't mean anything by it. He loves to tease. You should hear some of the things he says about my job—you'd think a travel agent did nothing but hand out brochures for the tropics."

Kelly's abrupt nod was unconvincing.

Mentally, Jo Marie decided to have a talk with her big brother. He shouldn't tease Kelly as if she were his sister. Kelly didn't know how to react to it. As the

youngest daughter of a large southern candy manu-
facturer, Kelly had been sheltered and pampered most
of her life. Her only brother was years older and apparently the age difference didn't allow for many sib-
ling conflicts. With four brothers, Jo Marie was no
stranger to family squabbles and could stand her own
against any one of them.

The apartment was a welcome sight after the
twenty-minute freeway drive. Jo Marie and Kelly
thought of it as their port in the storm. The two-floor
apartment buidling resembled the historic mansion
from *Gone With the Wind*. It maintained the flavor of
the Old South without the problem of constant repairs typical of many older buildings.

The minute they were in the door, Kelly headed for
her room. "If you don't mind I think I'll pack."

"Sure. Go ahead." Carelessly, Jo Marie kicked off
her low-heeled shoes. Slouching on the love seat, she
leaned her head back and closed her eyes. The strain
of the hectic rush hour traffic and the tension of a
busy day ebbed away with every relaxing breath.

The sound of running bathwater didn't surprise Jo
Marie. Kelly wanted to get an early start. Her family
lived in an ultramodern home along Lakeshore Drive.
The house bordered Lake Pontchartrain. Jo Marie
had been inside the Beaumont home only once. That
had been enough for her to realize just how good the
candy business was.

Jo Marie was sure that Charles Beaumont may have
disapproved of his only daughter moving into an
apartment with a "nobody" like her, but once he'd
learned that she was the great-great granddaughter of
Jubal Anderson Early, a Confederate Army colonel,
he'd sanctioned the move. Sometime during the Civil

War, Colonel Early had been instrumental in saving the life of a young Beaumont. Hence, a-hundred-and-some-odd years later, Early was a name to respect.

Humming Christmas music softly to herself, Jo Marie wandered into the kitchen and pulled the orange juice from the refrigerator shelf.

"Want a glass?" She held up the pitcher to Kelly who stepped from the bathroom, dressed in a short terry-cloth robe, with a thick towel securing her bouncy blond curls. One look at her friend and Jo Marie set the ceramic container on the kitchen counter.

"You've been crying." They'd lived together for three years, and apart from one sad, sentimental movie, Jo Marie had never seen Kelly cry.

"No, something's in my eye," she said and sniffled.

"Then why's your nose so red?"

"Maybe I'm catching a cold." She offered the weak explanation and turned sharply toward her room.

Jo Marie's smooth brow narrowed. This was Mark's doing. She was convinced he was the cause of Kelly's uncharacteristic display of emotion.

Something rang untrue about the whole situation between Kelly and Mark. Kelly wasn't a soft, southern belle who fainted at the least provocation. That was another teasing comment Mark enjoyed hurling at her. Kelly was a lady, but no shrinking violet. Jo Marie had witnessed Kelly in action, fighting for her patients and several political causes. The girl didn't back down often. After Thanksgiving, Jo Marie would help Kelly fine-tune a few witty comebacks. As Mark's sister, Jo Marie was well acquainted with her brother's weak spots. The only way to fight fire was

with fire she mused humorously. Together, Jo Marie
and Kelly would teach Mark a lesson.

"You want me to fix something to eat before you
head for your parents?" Jo Marie shouted from the
kitchen. She was standing in front of the cupboard,
scanning its meager contents. "How does soup and a
sandwich sound?"

"Boring," Kelly returned. "I'm not really hungry."

"Eight hours of back-breaking work on the surgical ward and you're not interested in food? Are you
having problems with your tonsils again?"

"I had them out, remember?"

Slowly, Jo Marie straightened. Yes, she remembered. All too well. It had been outside the hospital
that she'd literally run into the dream man. Unbidden
thoughts of him crowded her mind and forcefully she
shook her head to free herself of his image.

Jo Marie had fixed herself dinner and was sitting in
front of the television watching the evening news by
the time Kelly reappeared.

"I'm leaving now."

"Okay." Jo Marie didn't take her eyes off the television. "Have a happy Thanksgiving; don't eat too
much turkey and trimmings."

"Don't throw any wild parties while I'm away."
That was a small joke between them. Jo Marie rarely
dated these days. Not since—Mardi Gras. Kelly
couldn't understand this change in her friend and affectionately teased Jo Marie about her sudden lack of
an interesting social life.

"Oh, Kelly, before I forget—" Jo Marie gave her a
wicked smile "—bring back some pralines, would
you? After all, it's the holidays, so we can splurge."

At any other time Kelly would rant that she'd grown up with candy all her life and detested the sugary sweet concoction. Pralines were Jo Marie's weakness, but the candy would rot before Kelly would eat any of it.

"Sure, I'll be happy to," she agreed lifelessly and was gone before Jo Marie realized her friend had slipped away. Returning her attention to the news, Jo Marie was more determined than ever to have a talk with her brother.

The doorbell chimed at seven. Jo Marie was spreading a bright red polish on her toenails. She grumbled under her breath and screwed on the top of the bottle. But before she could answer the door, her brother strolled into the apartment and flopped down on the sofa that sat at right angles to the matching love seat.

"Come in and make yourself at home," Jo Marie commented dryly.

"I don't suppose you've got anything to eat around here." Dark brown eyes glanced expectantly into the kitchen. All five of the Early children shared the same dusty, dark eyes.

"This isn't a restaurant, you know."

"I know. By the way, where's money bags?"

"Who?" Confused, Jo Marie glanced up from her toes.

"Kelly."

Jo Marie didn't like the reference to Kelly's family wealth, but decided now wasn't the time to comment. Her brother worked long hours and had been out of sorts lately. "She's left for her parents' home already."

A soft snicker followed Jo Marie's announcement.

"Damn it, Mark, I wish you'd lay off Kelly. She's not used to being teased. It really bothers her."

"I'm only joking," Mark defended himself. "Kell knows that."

"I don't think she does. She was crying tonight and I'm sure it's your fault."

"Kelly crying?" He straightened and leaned forward, linking his hands. "But I was only kidding."

"That's the problem. You can't seem to let up on her. You're always putting her down one way or another."

Mark reached for a magazine, but not before Jo Marie saw that his mouth was pinched and hard. "She asks for it."

Rolling her eyes, Jo Marie continued adding the fire-engine-red color to her toes. It wouldn't do any good for her to argue with Mark. Kelly and Mark had to come to an agreement on their own. But that didn't mean Jo Marie couldn't hand Kelly ammunition now and again. Her brother had his vulnerable points, and Jo Marie would just make certain Kelly was aware of them. Then she could sit back and watch the sparks fly.

Busy with her polish, Jo Marie didn't notice for several minutes how quiet her brother had become. When she lifted her gaze to him, she saw that he had a pained, troubled look. His brow was furrowed in thought.

"I lost a child today," he announced tightly. "I couldn't understand it either. Not medically, I don't mean that. Anything can happen. She'd been brought in last week with a ruptured appendix. We knew from the beginning it was going to be touch and go." He paused and breathed in sharply. "But you know, deep down inside I believed she'd make it. She was their only daughter. The apple of her parents' eye. If all the love in that mother's heart couldn't hold back death's hand, then what good is medical science? What good am I?''

Mark had raised these questions before and Jo Marie had no answers. "I don't know," she admitted solemnly and reached out to touch his hand in reassurance. Mark didn't want to hear the pat answers. He couldn't see that now. Not when he felt like he'd failed this little girl and her parents in some obscure way. At times like these, she'd look at her brother who was a strong, committed doctor and see the doubt in his eyes. She had no answers. Sometimes she wasn't even sure she completely understood his questions.

After wiping his hand across his tired face, Mark stood. "I'm on duty tomorrow morning so I probably won't be at the folks' place until late afternoon. Tell Mom I'll try to make it on time. If I can't, the least you can do is to be sure and save a plate for me.''

Knowing Mark, he was likely to go without eating until tomorrow if left to his own devices. "Let me fix you something now," Jo Marie offered. From his unnatural pallor, Jo Marie surmised that Mark couldn't even remember when he'd eaten his last decent meal, coffee and a doughnut on the run excluded.

He glanced at his watch. "I haven't got time. Thanks anyway." Before she could object, he was at the door.

Why had he come? Jo Marie wondered absently. He'd done a lot of that lately—stopping in for a few minutes without notice. And it wasn't as if her apartment were close to the hospital. Mark had to go out of his way to visit her. With a bemused shrug, she followed him to the front door and watched as he sped away in that run-down old car he was so fond of driving. As he left, Jo Marie mentally questioned if her instincts had been on target all along and Kelly and Mark did hold some deep affection for each other. Mark hadn't come tonight for any specific reason. His first question had been about Kelly. Only later had he mentioned losing the child.

"Jo Marie," her mother called from the kitchen. "Would you mind mashing the potatoes?"

The large family kitchen was bustling with activity. The long white counter top was filled with serving bowls ready to be placed on the linen-covered dining room table. Sweet potato and pecan pies were cooling on the smaller kitchen table and the aroma of spice and turkey filled the house.

"Smells mighty good in here," Franklin Early proclaimed, sniffing appreciatively as he strolled into the kitchen and placed a loving arm around his wife's waist.

"Scat," Jo Marie's mother cried with a dismissive wave of her hand. "I won't have you in here sticking your fingers in the pies and blaming it on the boys. Dinner will be ready in ten minutes."

Mark arrived, red faced and slightly breathless. He kissed his mother on the cheek and when she wasn't looking, popped a sweet pickle into his mouth. "I hope I'm not too late."

"I'd say you had perfect timing," Jo Marie teased and handed him the electric mixer. "Here, mash these potatoes while I finish setting the table."

"No way, little sister." His mouth was twisted mockingly as he gave her back the appliance. "I'll set the table. No one wants lumpy potatoes."

The three younger boys, all in their teens, sat in front of the television watching a football game. The Early family enjoyed sports, especially football. Jo Marie's mother had despaired long ago that her only daughter would ever grow up properly. Instead of playing with dolls, her toys had been cowboy boots and little green army men. Touch football was as much a part of her life as ballet was for some girls.

With Mark out of the kitchen, Jo Marie's mother turned to her. "Have you been feeling all right lately?"

"Me?" The question caught her off guard. "I'm feeling fine. Why shouldn't I be?"

Ruth Early lifted one shoulder in a delicate shrug. "You've had a look in your eye lately." She turned and leaned her hip against the counter, her head tilted at a thoughtful angle. "The last time I saw that look was in your Aunt Bessie's eye before she was married. Tell me, Jo Marie, are you in love?"

Jo Marie hesitated, not knowing how to explain her feelings for a man she had met so briefly. He was more illusion than reality. Her own private fantasy. Those few moments with the dream man were beyond explaining, even to her own mother.

"No," she answered finally, making busy work by placing the serving spoons in the bowls.

"Is he married? Is that it? Save yourself a lot of grief, Jo Marie, and stay away from him if he is. You understand?"

"Yes," she murmured, her eyes avoiding her mother's. For all she knew he could well be married.

Not until late that night did Jo Marie let herself into her apartment. The day had been full. After the huge family dinner, they'd played cards until Mark trapped Jo Marie into playing a game of touch football for old times' sake. Jo Marie agreed and proved that she hadn't lost her "touch."

The apartment looked large and empty. Kelly stayed with her parents over any major holidays. Kelly's family seemed to feel that Kelly still belonged at home and always would, no matter what her age. Although Kelly was twenty-four, the apartment she shared with Jo Marie was more for convenience sake than any need to separate herself from her family.

With her mother's words echoing in her ear, Jo Marie sauntered into her bedroom and dressed for bed. Friday was a work day for her as it was for both Mark and Kelly. The downtown area of New Orleans would be hectic with Christmas shoppers hoping to pick up their gifts from the multitude of sales.

As a travel agent, Jo Marie didn't have many walk-in customers to deal with, but her phone rang continuously. Several people wanted to book holiday vacations, but there was little available that she could offer. The most popular vacation spots had been booked months in advance. Several times her information was accepted with an irritated grumble as if she were to blame. By the time she stepped off the bus outside her apartment, Jo Marie wasn't in any mood for company.

No sooner had the thought formed than she caught sight of her brother. He was parked in the lot outside the apartment building. Hungry and probably looking for a hot meal, she guessed. He knew that their mother had sent a good portion of the turkey and stuffing home with Jo Marie so Mark's appearance wasn't any real surprise.

"Hi," she said and knocked on his car window. The faraway look in his eyes convinced her that after all these years Mark had finally learned to sleep with his eyes open. He was so engrossed in his thoughts that Jo Marie was forced to tap on his window a second time.

"Paging Dr. Early," she mimicked in a high-pitched hospital voice. "Paging Dr. Mark Early."

Mark turned and stared at her blankly. "Oh, hi." He sat up and climbed out of the car.

"I suppose you want something to eat." Her greeting wasn't the least bit cordial, but she was tired and irritable.

The edge of Mark's mouth curled into a sheepish grin. "If it isn't too much trouble."

"No," she offered him an apologetic smile. "It's just been a rough day and my feet hurt."

"My sister sits in an office all day, files her nails, reads books and then complains that her feet hurt."

Jo Marie was too weary to rise to the bait. "Not even your acid tongue is going to get a rise out of me tonight."

"I know something that will," Mark returned smugly.

"Ha." From force of habit, Jo Marie kicked off her shoes and strolled into the kitchen.

"Wanna bet?"

"I'm not a betting person, especially after playing cards with you yesterday, but if you care to impress me, fire away." Crossing her arms, she leaned against the refrigerator door and waited.

"Kelly's engaged."

Jo Marie slowly shook her head in disbelief. "I didn't think you'd stoop to fabrications."

That familiar angry, hurt look stole into Mark's eyes. "It's true, I heard it from the horse's own mouth."

Lightly shaking her head from side to side to clear her thoughts, Jo Marie still came up with a blank. "But who?" Kelly wasn't going out with anyone seriously.

"Some cousin. Rich, no doubt," Mark said and straddled a kitchen chair. "She's got a diamond as big as a baseball. Must be hard for her to work with a rock that size weighing down her hand."

"A cousin?" New Orleans was full of Beaumonts, but none that Kelly had mentioned in particular. "I can't believe it," Jo Marie gasped. "She'd have said something to me."

"From what I understand, she tried to phone last night, but we were still at the folks' house. Just as well," Mark mumbled under his breath. "I'm not about to toast this engagement. First she plays at being nurse and now she wants to play at being a wife."

Mark's bitterness didn't register past the jolt of surprise that Jo Marie felt. "Kelly engaged," she repeated.

"You don't need to keep saying it," Mark snapped.

"Saying what?" A jubilant Kelly walked in the front door.

"Never mind," Mark said and slowly stood. "It's time for me to be going, I'll talk to you later."

"What about dinner?"

"There's someone I'd like you both to meet," Kelly announced.

Ignoring her, Mark turned to Jo Marie. "I've suddenly lost my appetite."

"Jo Marie, I'd like to introduce you to my fiancé, Andrew Beaumont."

Jo Marie's gaze swung from the frustrated look on her brother's face to an intense pair of gray eyes. There was only one man on earth with eyes the shade of a winter sea. The dream man.

Chapter Two

Stunned into speechlessness, Jo Marie struggled to maintain her composure. She took in a deep breath to calm her frantic heartbeat and forced a look of pleasant surprise. Andrew Beaumont apparently didn't even remember her. Jo Marie couldn't see so much as a flicker of recognition in the depth of his eyes. In the last nine months it was unlikely that he had given her more than a passing thought, if she'd been worthy of even that. And yet, she vividly remembered every detail of him, down to the crisp dark hair, the broad, muscular shoulders and faint twist of his mouth.

With an effort that was just short of superhuman, Jo Marie smiled. "Congratulations, you two. But what a surprise."

Kelly hurried across the room and hugged her tightly. "It was to us, too. Look." She held out her hand for Jo Marie to admire the flashing diamond. Mark hadn't been exaggerating. The flawless gem mounted in an antique setting was the largest Jo Marie had ever seen.

"What did I tell you," Mark whispered in her ear.

Confused, Kelly glanced from sister to brother. "Drew and I are celebrating tonight. We'd love it if you came. Both of you."

"No," Jo Marie and Mark declared in unison.

"I'm bushed," Jo Marie begged off.

"...and tired," Mark finished lamely.

For the first time, Andrew spoke. "We insist." The deep, resonant voice was exactly as Jo Marie remembered. But tonight there was something faintly arrogant in the way he spoke that dared Jo Marie and Mark to put up an argument.

Brother and sister exchanged questioning glances, neither willing to be drawn into the celebration. Each for their own reasons, Jo Marie mused.

"Well—" Mark cleared his throat, clearly ill at ease with the formidable fiancé "—perhaps another time."

"You're Jo Marie's brother?" Andrew asked with a mocking note.

"How'd you know?"

Kelly stuck her arm through Andrew's. "Family resemblance, silly. No one can look at the two of you and not know you're related."

"I can't say the same thing about you two. I thought it was against the law to marry a cousin." Mark didn't bother to disguise his contempt.

"We're distant cousins," Kelly explained brightly. Her eyes looked adoringly into Andrew's and Jo Marie felt her stomach tighten. Jealousy. This sickening feeling in the pit of her stomach was the green-eyed monster. Jo Marie had only experienced brief tastes of the emotion; now it filled her mouth until she thought she would choke on it.

"I...had a horribly busy day." Jo Marie sought frantically for an excuse to stay home.

"And I'd have to go home and change," Mark added, looking down over his pale gray cords and sport shirt.

"No, you wouldn't," Kelly contradicted with a provocative smile. "We're going to K-Paul's."

"Sure, and wait in line half the night." A muscle twitched in Mark's jaw.

K-Paul's was a renowned restaurant that was ranked sixth in the world. Famous, but not elegant. The small establishment served creole cooking at its best.

"No," Kelly supplied, and the dip in her voice revealed how much she wanted to share this night with her friends. "Andrew's a friend of Paul's."

Mark looked at Jo Marie and rolled his eyes. "I should have known," he muttered sarcastically.

"What time did you say we'd be there, darling?"

Jo Marie closed her eyes to the sharp flash of pain at the affectionate term Kelly used so freely. These jealous sensations were crazy. She had no right to feel this way. This man...Andrew Beaumont, was a blown-up figment of her imagination. The brief moments they shared should have been forgotten long ago. Kelly was her friend. Her best friend. And Kelly deserved every happiness.

With a determined jut to her chin, Jo Marie flashed her roommate a warm smile. "Mark and I would be honored to join you tonight."

"We would?" Mark didn't sound pleased. Irritation rounded his dark eyes and he flashed Jo Marie a look that openly contradicted her agreement. Jo Marie wanted to tell him that he owed Kelly this much for all the teasing he'd given her. In addition, her look pleaded with him to understand how much she needed his support tonight. Saying as much was impossible, but she hoped her eyes conveyed the message.

Jo Marie turned slightly so that she faced the tall figure standing only a few inches from her. "It's generous of you to include us," she murmured, but discovered that she was incapable of meeting Andrew's penetrating gaze.

"Give us a minute to freshen up and we'll be on our way," Kelly's effervescent enthusiasm filled the room. "Come on, Jo Marie."

The two men remained in the compact living room. Jo Marie glanced back to note that Mark looked like a jaguar trapped in an iron cage. When he wasn't pacing, he stood restlessly shifting his weight repeatedly from one foot to the other. His look was weary and there was an uncharacteristic tightness to his mouth that narrowed his eyes.

"What do you think," Kelly whispered, and gave a long sigh. "Isn't he fantastic? I think I'm the luckiest girl in the world. Of course, we'll have to wait until after the holidays to make our announcement official. But isn't Drew wonderful?"

Jo Marie forced a noncommittal nod. The raw disappointment left an aching void in her heart. Andrew should have been hers. "He's wonderful." The words came out sounding more like a tortured whisper than a compliment.

Kelly paused, lowering the brush. "Jo, are you all right? You sound like you're going to cry."

"Maybe I am." Tears burned for release, but not for the reason Kelly assumed. "It's not every day I lose my best friend."

"But you're not losing me."

Jo Marie's fingers curved around the cold bathroom sink. "But you are planning to get married?"

"Oh yes, we'll make an official announcement in January, but we haven't set a definite date for the wedding."

That surprised Jo Marie. Andrew didn't look like the kind of man who would encourage a long engagement. She would have thought that once he'd made a decision, he'd move on it. But then, she didn't know Andrew Beaumont. Not really.

A glance in the mirror confirmed that her cheeks were pale, her dark eyes haunted with a wounded, perplexed look. A quick application of blush added color to her bloodless face, but there was little she could do to disguise the troubled look in her eyes. She could only pray that no one would notice.

"Ready?" Kelly stood just outside the open door.

Jo Marie's returning smile was frail as she mentally braced herself for the coming ordeal. She paused long enough to dab perfume to the pulse points at the hollow of her neck and at her wrists.

"I, for one, am starved," Kelly announced as they returned to the living room. "And from what I remember of K-Paul's, eating is an experience we won't forget."

Jo Marie was confident that every part of this evening would be indelibly marked in her memory, but not for the reasons Kelly assumed.

Andrew's deep blue Mercedes was parked beside Mark's old clunker. The differences between the two men were as obvious as the vehicles they drove.

Clearly ill at ease, Mark stood on the sidewalk in front of his car. "Why don't Jo Marie and I follow you?"

"Nonsense," Kelly returned, "there's plenty of room in Drew's car for everyone. You know what the traffic is like. We could get separated. I wouldn't want that to happen."

Mark's twisted mouth said that he would have given a weeks' pay to suddenly disappear. Jo Marie studied her brother carefully from her position in the back seat. His displeasure at being included in this evening's celebration was confusing. There was far more than reluctance in his attitude. He might not get along with Kelly, but she would have thought that Mark would wish Kelly every happiness. But he didn't. Not by the stiff, unnatural behavior she'd witnessed from him tonight.

Mark's attitude didn't change any at the restaurant. Paul, the robust chef, came out from the kitchen and greeted the party himself.

After they'd ordered, the small party sat facing one another in stony silence. Kelly made a couple of attempts to start up the conversation, but her efforts were to no avail. The two men eyed each other, looking as if they were ready to do battle at the slightest provocation.

Several times while they ate their succulent Shrimp Remoulade, Jo Marie found her gaze drawn to Andrew. In many ways he was exactly as she remembered. In others, he was completely different. His voice was low pitched and had a faint drawl. And he wasn't a talker. His expression was sober almost to the point of being somber, which was unusual for a man celebrating his engagement. Another word that her mind tossed out was disillusioned. Andrew Beaumont looked as though he was disenchanted with life. From everything she'd learned he was wealthy and successful. He owned a land development firm. Delta Development, Inc. had been in the Beaumont family for three generations. According to Kelly, the firm had expanded extensively under Andrew's direction.

But if Jo Marie was paying attention to Andrew, he was nothing more than polite to her. He didn't acknowledge her with anything more than an occasional look. And since she hadn't directed any questions to him, he hadn't spoken either. At least not to her.

Paul's special touch for creole cooking made the meal memorable. And although her thoughts were troubled and her heart perplexed, when the waitress took Jo Marie's plate away she had done justice to the meal. Even Mark, who had sat uncommunicative and sullen through most of the dinner, had left little on his plate.

After K-Paul's, Kelly insisted they visit the French Quarter. The others were not as enthusiastic. After an hour of walking around and sampling some of the best jazz sounds New Orleans had to offer, they returned to the apartment.

"I'll make the coffee," Kelly proposed as they climbed from the luxury car.

Mark made a show of glancing at his watch. "I think I'll skip the chicory," he remarked in a flippant tone. "Tomorrow's a busy day."

"Come on, Mark—" Kelly pouted prettily "—don't be a spoil sport."

Mark's face darkened with a scowl. "If you insist."

"It isn't every day I celebrate my engagement. And, Mark, have you noticed that we haven't fought once all night? That must be some kind of a record."

A poor facsimile of a smile lifted one corner of his mouth. "It must be," he agreed wryly. He lagged behind as they climbed the stairs to the second-story apartment.

Jo Marie knew her brother well enough to know he'd have the coffee and leave as soon as it was polite to do so.

They sat in stilted silence, drinking their coffee.

"Do you two work together?" Andrew directed his question to Jo Marie.

Flustered she raised her palm to her breast. "Me?"

"Yes. Did you and Kelly meet at Tulane Hospital?"

"No, I'm a travel agent. Mark's the one in the family with the brains." She heard the breathlessness in her voice and hoped that he hadn't.

"Don't put yourself down," Kelly objected. "You're no dummy. Did you know that Jo Marie is actively involved in saving our wetlands? She volunteers her time as an office worker for the Land For The Future organization."

"That doesn't require intelligence, only time," Jo Marie murmured self-consciously and congratulated herself for keeping her voice even.

For the first time that evening, Andrew directed his attention to her and smiled. The effect it had on Jo Marie's pulse was devastating. To disguise her reaction, she raised the delicate china cup to her lips and took a tentative sip of the steaming coffee.

"And all these years I thought the LFTF was for little old ladies."

"No." Jo Marie was able to manage only the one word.

"At one time Jo Marie wanted to be a biologist," Kelly supplied.

Andrew arched two thick brows. "What stopped you?"

"Me," Mark cut in defensively. "The schooling she required was extensive and our parents couldn't afford to pay for us both to attend university at the same time. Jo Marie decided to drop out."

"That's not altogether true." Mark was making her sound noble and self-sacrificing. "It wasn't like that. If I'd wanted to continue my schooling there were lots of ways I could have done so."

"And you didn't?" Again Andrew's attention was focused on her.

She moistened her dry lips before continuing. "No. I plan to go back to school someday. Until then I'm staying active in the causes that mean the most to me and to the future of New Orleans."

"Jo Marie's our neighborhood scientist," Kelly added proudly. "She has a science club for children every other Saturday morning. I swear she's a natural with those kids. She's always taking them on hikes and planning field trips for them."

"You must like children." Again Andrew's gaze slid to Jo Marie.

"Yes," she answered self-consciously and lowered her eyes. She was grateful when the topic of conversation drifted to other subjects. When she chanced a look at Andrew, she discovered that his gaze centered on her lips. It took a great deal of restraint not to moisten them. And even more to force the memory of his kiss from her mind.

Once again, Mark made a show of looking at his watch and standing. "The evening's been—" he faltered looking for an adequate description "—interesting. Nice meeting you, Beaumont. Best wishes to you and Florence Nightingale."

The sip of coffee stuck in Jo Marie's throat, causing a moment of intense pain until her muscles relaxed enough to allow her to swallow. Grateful that no one had noticed, Jo Marie set her cup aside and walked with her brother to the front door. "I'll talk to you later," she said in farewell.

Mark wiped a hand across his eyes. He looked more tired than Jo Marie could remember seeing him in a long time. "I've been dying to ask you all night. Isn't Kelly's rich friend the one who filled in the swampland for that housing development you fought so hard against?"

"And lost." Jo Marie groaned inwardly. She had been a staunch supporter of the environmentalists and had helped gather signatures against the project. But to no avail. "Then he's also the one who bought out Rose's," she murmured thoughtfully as a feeling of dread washed over her. Rose's Hotel was in the French Quarter and was one of the landmarks of Louisiana. In addition to being a part of New Orleans' history, the hotel was used to house transients. It was true that Rose's was badly in need of repairs, but Jo Marie hated to see the wonderful old building destroyed in the name of progress. If annihilating the breeding habitat of a hundred different species of birds hadn't troubled Andrew Beaumont, then she doubted that an old hotel in ill-repair would matter to him either.

Rubbing her temple to relieve an unexpected and throbbing headache, Jo Marie nodded. "I remember Kelly saying something about a cousin being responsible for Rose's. But I hadn't put the two together."

"He has," Mark countered disdainfully. "And come up with megabucks. Our little Kelly has reeled in quite a catch, if you like the cold, heartless sort."

Jo Marie's mind immediately rejected that thought. Andrew Beaumont may be the man responsible for several controversial land acquisitions, but he wasn't heartless. Five minutes with him at the Mardi Gras had proven otherwise.

Mark's amused chuckle carried into the living room. "You've got that battle look in your eye. What are you thinking?"

"Nothing," she returned absently. But already her mind was racing furiously. "I'll talk to you tomorrow."

"I'll give you a call," Mark promised and was gone.

When Jo Marie returned to the living room, she found Kelly and Andrew chatting companionably. They paused and glanced at her as she rejoined them.

"You've known each other for a long time, haven't you?" Jo Marie lifted the half-full china cup, making an excuse to linger. She sat on the arm of the love seat, unable to decide if she should stay and speak her mind or repress her tongue.

"We've known each other since childhood." Kelly answered for the pair.

"And Andrew is the distant cousin you said had bought Rose's."

Kelly's sigh was uncomfortable. "I was hoping you wouldn't put two and two together."

"To be honest, I didn't. Mark figured it out."

A frustrated look tightened Kelly's once happy features.

"Will someone kindly tell me what you two are talking about?" Andrew asked.

"Rose's," they chimed in unison.

"Rose's," he repeated slowly and a frown appeared between his gray eyes.

Apparently Andrew Beaumont had so much land one small hotel didn't matter.

"The hotel."

The unexpected sharpness in his voice caused Jo Marie to square her shoulders. "It may seem like a little thing to you."

"Not for what that piece of land cost me," he countered in a hard voice.

"I don't think Drew likes to mix business with pleasure," Kelly warned, but Jo Marie disregarded the well-intended advice.

"But the men living in Rose's will have nowhere to go."

"They're bums."

A sadness filled her at the insensitive way he referred to these men. "Rose's had housed homeless men for twenty years. These men need someplace where they can get a hot meal and can sleep."

"It's a prime location for luxury condominiums," he said cynically.

"But what about the transients? What will become of them?"

"That, Miss Early, is no concern of mine."

Unbelievably Jo Marie felt tears burn behind her eyes. She blinked them back. Andrew Beaumont wasn't the dream man she'd fantasized over all these months. He was cold and cynical. The only love he had in his life was profit. A sadness settled over her with a weight she thought would be crippling.

"I feel very sorry for you, Mr. Beaumont," she said smoothly, belying her turbulent emotions. "You may be very rich, but there's no man poorer than one who has no tolerance for the weakness of others."

Kelly gasped softly and groaned. "I knew this was going to happen."

"Are you always so opinionated, Miss Early?" There was no disguising the icy tones.

"No, but there are times when things are so wrong that I can't remain silent." She turned to Kelly. "I apologize if I've ruined your evening. If you'll excuse me now, I think I'll go to bed. Good night, Mr. Beaumont. May you and Kelly have many years of happiness together." The words nearly stuck in her throat but she managed to get them out before walking from the room.

"If this offends you in any way I won't do it." Jo Marie studied her roommate carefully. The demonstration in front of Rose's had been planned weeks ago. Jo Marie's wooden picket sign felt heavy in her hand. For the first time in her life, her convictions conflicted with her feelings. She didn't want to march against Andrew. It didn't matter what he'd done, but she couldn't stand by and see those poor men turned into the streets, either. Not in the name of progress. Not when progress was at the cost of the less fortunate and the fate of a once lovely hotel.

"This picket line was arranged long before you met Drew."

"That hasn't got anything to do with this. Drew is important to you. I wouldn't want to do something that will place your relationship with him in jeopardy.''

"It won't."

Kelly sounded far more confident than Jo Marie felt.

"In fact," she continued, "I doubt that Drew even knows anything about the demonstration. Those things usually do nothing to sway his decision. In fact, I'd say they do more harm than good as far as he's concerned."

Jo Marie had figured that much out herself, but she couldn't stand by doing nothing. Rose's was scheduled to be shut down the following week...a short month before Christmas. Jo Marie didn't know how anyone could be so heartless. The hotel was to be torn down a week later and new construction was scheduled to begin right after the first of the year.

Kelly paused at the front door while Jo Marie picked up her picket sign and tossed the long strap of her purse over her shoulder.

"You do understand why I can't join you?" she asked hesitatingly.

"Of course," Jo Marie said and exhaled softly. She'd never expected Kelly to participate. This fight couldn't include her friend without causing bitter feelings.

"Be careful." Her arms wrapped around her waist to chase away a chill, Kelly walked down to the parking lot with Jo Marie.

"Don't worry. This is a peaceful demonstration. The only wounds I intend to get are from carrying this sign. It's heavy."

Cocking her head sideways, Kelly read the sign for the tenth time. Save Rose's Hotel. A Piece Of New

Orleans History. Kelly chuckled and slowly shook her
head. "I should get a picture of you. Drew would get
a real kick out of that."

The offer of a picture was a subtle reminder that
Drew wouldn't so much as see the sign. He probably
wasn't even aware of the protest rally.

Friends of Rose's and several others from the Land
For The Future headquarters were gathered outside
the hotel when Jo Marie arrived. Several people who
knew Jo Marie raised their hands in welcome.

"Have the television and radio stations been notified?" the organizer asked a tall man Jo Marie didn't
recognize.

"I notified them, but most weren't all that interested. I doubt that we'll be given air time."

A feeling of gloom settled over the group. An unexpected cloudburst did little to brighten their mood.
Jo Marie hadn't brought her umbrella and was
drenched in minutes. A chill caused her teeth to chat-
ter and no matter how hard she tried, she couldn't stop
shivering. Uncaring, the rain fell indiscriminately over
the small group of protesters.

"You little fool," Mark said when he found her an
hour later. "Are you crazy, walking around wet and
cold like that?" His voice was a mixture of exaspera-
tion and pride.

"I'm making a statement," Jo Marie argued.

"You're right. You're telling the world what a fool
you are. Don't you have any better sense than this?"

Jo Marie ignored him, placing one foot in front of
the other as she circled the sidewalk in front of Rose's
Hotel.

"Do you think Beaumont cares?"

Jo Marie refused to be drawn into his argument. "Instead of arguing with me, why don't you go inside and see what's holding up the coffee?"

"You're going to need more than a hot drink to prevent you from getting pneumonia. Listen to reason for once in your life."

"No!" Emphatically Jo Marie stamped her foot. "This is too important."

"And your health isn't?"

"Not now." The protest group had dwindled down to less than ten. "I'll be all right." She shifted the sign from one shoulder to the other and flexed her stiff fingers. Her back ached from the burden of her message. And with every step the rain water in her shoes squished noisily. "I'm sure we'll be finished in another hour."

"If you aren't, I'm carting you off myself," Mark shouted angrily and returned to his car. He shook his finger at her in warning as he drove past.

True to his word, Mark returned an hour later and followed her back to the apartment.

Jo Marie could hardly drive she was shivering so violently. Her long chestnut hair fell in limp tendrils over her face. Rivulets of cold water ran down her neck and she bit into her bottom lip at the pain caused by gripping the steering wheel. Carrying the sign had formed painful blisters in the palms of her hands. This was one protest rally she wouldn't soon forget.

Mark seemed to blame Andrew Beaumont for the fact that she was cold, wet and miserable. But it wasn't Andrew's fault that it had rained. Not a single forecaster had predicted it would. She'd lived in New Orleans long enough to know she should carry an umbrella with her. Mark was looking for an excuse to dislike Andrew. Any excuse. In her heart, Jo Marie couldn't. No matter what he'd done, there was something deep within her that wouldn't allow any bitterness inside. In some ways she was disillusioned and hurt that her dream man wasn't all she'd thought. But that was as deep as her resentments went.

"Little fool," Mark repeated tenderly as he helped her out of the car. "Let's get you upstairs and into a hot bath."

"As long as I don't have to listen to you lecture all night," she said, her teeth chattering as she climbed the stairs to the second-story apartment. Although she was thoroughly miserable, there was a spark of humor in her eyes as she opened the door and stepped inside the apartment.

"Jo Marie," Kelly cried in alarm. "Good grief, what happened?"

A light laugh couldn't disguise her shivering. "Haven't you looked out the window lately? It's raining cats and dogs."

"This is your fault, Beaumont," Mark accused harshly and Jo Marie sucked in a surprised breath. In her misery, she hadn't noticed Andrew, who was casually sitting on the love seat.

He rose to a standing position and glared at Mark as if her brother were a mad man. "Explain yourself," he demanded curtly.

Kelly intervened, crossing the room and placing a hand on Andrew's arm. "Jo Marie was marching in that rally I was telling you about."

"In front of Rose's Hotel," Mark added, his fists tightly clenched at his side. He looked as if he wanted to get physical. Consciously, Jo Marie moved closer to her brother's side. Fist fighting was so unlike Mark.

He was a healer, not a boxer. One look told Jo Marie that in a physical exchange, Mark would lose.

Andrew's mouth twisted scornfully. "You, my dear Miss Early, are a fool."

Jo Marie dipped her head mockingly. "And you, Mr. Beaumont, are heartless."

"But rich," Mark intervened. "And money goes a long way in making a man attractive. Isn't that right, Kelly?"

Kelly went visibly pale, her blue eyes filling with tears. "That's not true," she cried, her words jerky as she struggled for control.

"You will apologize for that remark, Early." Andrew's low voice held a threat that was undeniable.

Mark knotted and unknotted his fists. "I won't apologize for the truth. If you want to step outside, maybe you'd like to make something of it."

"Mark!" Both Jo Marie and Kelly gasped in shocked disbelief.

Jo Marie moved first. "Get out of here before you cause trouble." Roughly she opened the door and shoved him outside.

"You heard what I said," Mark growled on his way out the door.

"I've never seen Mark behave like that," Jo Marie murmured, her eyes lowered to the carpet where a small pool of water had formed. "I can only apologize." She paused and inhaled deeply. "And, Kelly, I'm sure you know he didn't mean what he said to you. He's upset because of the rally." Her voice was deep with emotion as she excused herself and headed for the bathroom.

A hot bath went a long way toward making her more comfortable. Mercifully, Andrew was gone by the time she had finished. She didn't feel up to another confrontation with him.

"Call on line three."

Automatically Jo Marie punched in the button and reached for her phone. "Jo Marie Early, may I help you?"

"You won."

"Mark?" He seldom phoned her at work.

"Did you hear me?" he asked excitedly.

"What did I win?" she asked humoring him.

"Beaumont."

Jo Marie's hand tightened around the receiver. "What do you mean?"

"It just came over the radio. Delta Development, Inc. is donating Rose's Hotel to the city," Mark announced with a short laugh. "Can you believe it?"

"Yes," Jo Marie closed her eyes to the onrush of emotion. Her dream man hadn't let her down. "I can believe it."

Chapter Three

But you must come," Kelly insisted, sitting across from Jo Marie. "It'll be miserable without you."

"Kell, I don't know." Jo Marie looked up from the magazine she was reading and nibbled on her lower lip.

"It's just a Christmas party with a bunch of stuffy people I don't know. You know how uncomfortable I am meeting new people. I hate parties."

"Then why attend?"

"Drew says we must. I'm sure he doesn't enjoy the party scene any more than I do, but he's got to go or offend a lot of business acquaintances."

"But I wasn't included in the invitation," Jo Marie argued. She'd always liked people and usually did well at social functions.

"Of course you were included. Both you and Mark," Kelly insisted. "Drew saw to that."

Thoughtfully, Jo Marie considered her roommate's request. As much as she objected, she really would like to go, if for no more reason than to thank Andrew for his generosity regarding Rose's. Although she'd seen him briefly a couple of times since, the opportunity hadn't presented itself to express her appreciation. The party was one way she could do that. New Orleans was famous for its festive balls and holiday parties. Without Kelly's invitation, Jo Marie doubted that there would ever be the chance for her to attend such an elaborate affair.

"All right," she conceded, "but I doubt that Mark will come." Mark and Andrew hadn't spoken since the last confrontation in the girls' living room. The air had hung heavy between them then and Jo Marie doubted that Andrew's decision regarding Rose's Hotel would change her brother's attitude.

"Leave Mark to me," Kelly said confidently. "Just promise me that you'll be there."

"I'll need a dress." Mentally Jo Marie scanned the contents of her closet and came up with zero. Nothing she owned would be suitable for such an elaborate affair.

"Don't worry, you can borrow something of mine," Kelly offered with a generosity that was innate to her personality.

Jo Marie nearly choked on her laughter. "I'm three inches taller than you." And several pounds heavier, but she preferred not to mention that. Only once before had Jo Marie worn Kelly's clothes. The night she'd met Andrew.

Kelly giggled and the bubbly sound was pleasant to the ears. "I heard miniskirts were coming back into style."

"Perhaps, but I doubt that the fashion will arrive in time for Christmas. Don't worry about me, I'll go out this afternoon and pick up some material for a dress."

"But will you have enough time between now and the party to sew it?" Kelly's blue eyes rounded with doubt.

"I'll make time." Jo Marie was an excellent seamstress. She had her mother to thank for that. Ruth Early had insisted that her only daughter learn to sew. Jo Marie had balked in the beginning. Her interests were anything but domestic. But now, as she had been several times in the past, she was grateful for the skill.

She found a pattern of a three-quarter-length dress with a matching jacket. The simplicity of the design made the outfit all the more appealing. Jo Marie could dress it either up or down, depending on the occasion. The silky, midnight blue material she purchased was perfect for the holiday, and Jo Marie knew that shade to be one of her better colors.

When she returned to the apartment, Kelly was gone. A note propped on the kitchen table explained that she wouldn't be back until dinner time.

After washing, drying, and carefully pressing the material, Jo Marie laid it out on the table for cutting. Intent on her task, she had pulled her hair away from her face and had tied it at the base of her neck with a rubber band. Straight pins were pressed between her lips when the doorbell chimed. The neighborhood children often stopped in for a visit. Usually Jo Marie welcomed their company, but she was busy now and interruptions could result in an irreparable mistake. She toyed with the idea of not answering.

The impatient buzz told her that her company was irritated at being kept waiting.

"Damn, damn, damn," she grumbled beneath her breath as she made her way across the room. Extracting the straight pins from her mouth, she stuck them in the small cushion she wore around her wrist.

"Andrew!" Secretly she thanked God the pins were out of her mouth or she would have swallowed them in her surprise.

"Is Kelly here?"

"No, but come in." Her heart was racing madly as he walked into the room. Nervous fingers tugged the rubber band from her chestnut hair in a futile attempt to look more presentable. She shook her hair free, then wished she'd kept it neatly in place. For days Jo Marie would have welcomed the opportunity to thank Andrew, but she discovered as she followed him into the living room that her tongue was tied and her mouth felt gritty and dry. "I'm glad you're here...I wanted to thank you for your decision about Rose's...the hotel."

He interrupted her curtly. "My dear Miss Early, don't be misled. My decision wasn't—"

Her hand stopped him. "I know," she said softly. He didn't need to tell her his reasoning. She was already aware it wasn't because of the rally or anything that she'd done or said. "I just wanted to thank you for whatever may have been your reason."

Their eyes met and held from across the room. Countless moments passed in which neither spoke. The air was electric between them and the urge to reach out and touch Andrew was almost overwhelming. The same breathlessness that had attacked her the night of the Mardi Gras returned. Andrew had to remember, he had to. Yet he gave no indication that he did.

Jo Marie broke eye contact first, lowering her gaze to the wool carpet. "I'm not sure where Kelly is, but she said she'd be back by dinner time." Her hand shook as she handed him the note off the kitchen counter.

"Kelly mentioned the party?"

Jo Marie nodded.

"You'll come?"

She nodded her head in agreement. "If I finish sewing this dress in time." She spoke so he wouldn't think she'd suddenly lost the ability to talk. Never had she been more aware of a man. Her heart was hammering at his nearness. He was so close all she had to do was reach out and touch him. But insurmountable barriers stood between them. At last, after all these months she was alone with her dream man. So many times a similar scene had played in her mind. But Andrew didn't remember her. The realization produced an indescribable ache in her heart. What had been the most profound moment in her life had been nothing to him.

"Would you like to sit down?" she offered, remembering her manners. "There's coffee on if you'd like a cup."

He shook his head. "No, thanks." He ran his hand along the top of the blue cloth that was stretched across the kitchen table. His eyes narrowed and he looked as if his thoughts were a thousand miles away.

"Why don't you buy a dress?"

A smile trembled at the edge of her mouth. To a man who had always had money, buying something as simple as a dress would seem the most logical solution.

"I sew most of my own things," she explained softly, rather than enlightening him with a lecture on economics.

"Did you make this?" His fingers touched the short sleeve of her cotton blouse and brushed against the sensitive skin of her upper arm.

Immediately a warmth spread where his fingers had come into contact with her flesh. Jo Marie's pale cheeks instantly flushed with a crimson flood of color. "Yes," she admitted hoarsely, hating the way her body, her voice, everything about her, was affected by this man.

"You do beautiful work."

She kept her eyes lowered and drew in a steadying breath. "Thank you."

"Next weekend I'll be having a Christmas party at my home for the employees of my company. I would be honored if both you and your brother attended."

Already her heart was racing with excitement; she'd love to visit his home. But seeing where he lived was only an excuse. She'd do anything to see more of him. "I can't speak for Mark," she answered after several moments, feeling guilty for her thoughts.

"But you'll come?"

"I'd be happy to. Thank you." Her only concern was that no one from Delta Development would recognize her as the same woman who was active in the protest against the housing development and in saving Rose's Hotel.

"Good," he said gruffly.

The curve of her mouth softened into a smile. "I'll tell Kelly that you were by. Would you like her to phone you?"

"No, I'll be seeing her later. Goodbye, Jo Marie."

She walked with him to the door, holding onto the knob longer than necessary. "Goodbye, Andrew," she murmured.

Jo Marie leaned against the door and covered her face with both hands. She shouldn't be feeling this eager excitement, this breathless bewilderment, this softness inside at the mere thought of him. Andrew Beaumont was her roommate's fiancé. She had to remember that. But somehow, Jo Marie recognized that her conscience could repeat the information all day, but it would have little effect on her restless heart.

The sewing machine was set up at the table when Kelly walked into the apartment a couple of hours later.

"I'm back," Kelly murmured happily as she hung her sweater in the closet.

"Where'd you go?"

"To see a friend."

Jo Marie thought she detected a note of hesitancy in her roommate's voice and glanced up momentarily from her task. She paused herself, then said, "Andrew was by."

A look of surprise worked its way across Kelly's pixie face. "Really? Did he say what he wanted?"

"Not really. He didn't leave a message." Jo Marie strove for nonchalance, but her fingers shook slightly and she hoped that her friend didn't notice the telltale mannerism.

"You like Drew, don't you?"

For some reason, Jo Marie's mind had always referred to him as Andrew. "Yes." She continued with the mechanics of sewing, but she could feel Kelly's eyes roam over her face as she studied her. Immediately a guilty flush reddened her cheeks. Somehow, some way, Kelly had detected how strongly Jo Marie felt about Andrew.

"I'm glad," Kelly said at last. "I'd like it if you two would fall in..." She hesitated before concluding with, "Never mind."

The two words were repeated in her mind like the dwindling sounds of an echo off canyon walls.

The following afternoon, Jo Marie arrived home from work and took a crisp apple from the bottom shelf of the refrigerator. She wanted a snack before pulling out her sewing machine again. Kelly was working late and had phoned her at the office so Jo Marie wouldn't worry. Holding the apple between her teeth, she lugged the heavy sewing machine out of the bedroom. No sooner had she set the case on top of the table than the doorbell chimed.

Releasing a frustrated sigh, she swallowed the bite of apple.

"Sign here, please." A clipboard was shoved under her nose.

"I beg your pardon," Jo Marie asked.

"I'm making a delivery, lady. Sign here."

"Oh." Maybe Kelly had ordered something without telling her. Quickly, she penned her name along the bottom line.

"Wait here," was the next abrupt instruction.

Shrugging her shoulder, Jo Marie leaned against the door jamb as the brusque man returned to the brown truck parked below and brought up two large boxes.

"Merry Christmas, Miss Early," he said with a sheepish grin as he handed her the delivery.

"Thank you." The silver box was the trademark of New Orleans' most expensive boutique. Gilded lettering wrote out the name of the proprietor, Madame

Renaux Marceau, across the top. Funny, Jo Marie couldn't recall Kelly saying she'd bought something there. But with the party coming, Kelly had apparently opted for the expensive boutique.

Dutifully Jo Marie carried the boxes into Kelly's room and set them on the bed. As she did so the shipping order attached to the smaller box, caught her eye. The statement was addressed to her, not Kelly.

Inhaling a jagged breath, Jo Marie searched the order blank to find out who would be sending her anything. Her parents could never have afforded something from Madame Renaux Marceau.

The air was sucked from her lungs as Jo Marie discovered Andrew Beaumont's name. She fumbled with the lids, peeled back sheer paper and gasped at the beauty of what lay before her. The full-length blue dress was the same midnight shade as the one she was sewing. But this gown was unlike anything Jo Marie had ever seen. A picture of Christmas, a picture of elegance. She held it up and felt tears prickle the back of her eyes. The bodice was layered with intricate rows of tiny pearls that formed a V at the waist. The gown was breathtakingly beautiful. Never had Jo Marie thought to own anything so perfect or so lovely. The second box contained a matching cape with an ornate display of tiny pearls.

Very carefully, Jo Marie folded the dress and cape and placed them back into the boxes. An ache inside her heart erupted into a broken sob. She wasn't a charity case. Did Andrew assume that because she sewed her own clothes that what she was making for the party would be unpresentable?

The telephone book revealed the information she needed. Following her instincts, Jo Marie grabbed a sweater and rushed out the door. She didn't stop until she pulled up in front of the large brick building with the gold plaque in the front that announced that this was the headquarters for Delta Development, Inc.

A listing of offices in the foyer told her where Andrew's was located. Jo Marie rode the elevator to the third floor. Most of the building was deserted, only a few employees remained. Those that did gave her curious stares, but no one questioned her presence.

The office door that had Andrew's name lettered on it was closed, but that didn't dissuade Jo Marie. His receptionist was placing the cover over her typewriter when Jo Marie barged inside.

"I'd like to see Mr. Beaumont," she demanded in a breathless voice.

The gray-haired receptionist glanced at the boxes under Jo Marie's arms and shook her head. "I'm sorry, but the office is closed for the day."

Jo Marie caught the subtle difference. "I didn't ask about the office. I said I wanted to see Mr. Beaumont." Her voice rose with her frustration.

A connecting door between two rooms opened. "Is there a problem, Mrs. Stewart?"

"I was just telling..."

"Jo Marie." Andrew's voice was an odd mixture of surprise and gruffness, yet gentle. His narrowed look centered on the boxes clasped under each arm. "Is there a problem?"

"As a matter of fact there is," she said, fighting to disguise the anger that was building within her to volcanic proportions.

Andrew stepped aside to admit her into his office.

"Will you be needing me further?" Jo Marie heard his secretary ask.

"No, thank you, Mrs. Stewart. I'll see you in the morning."

No sooner had Andrew stepped in the door than Jo Marie whirled on him. The silver boxes from the boutique sat squarely in the middle of Andrew's huge oak desk.

"I think you should understand something right now, Mr. Beaumont," she began heatedly, not bothering to hold back her annoyance. "I am not Cinderella and you most definitely are not my fairy godfather."

"Would I be amiss to guess that my gift displeases you?"

Jo Marie wanted to scream at him for being so calm. She cut her long nails into her palms in an effort to disguise her irritation. "If I am an embarrassment to you wearing a dress I've sewn myself, then I'll simply not attend your precious party."

He looked shocked.

"And furthermore, I am no one's poor relation."

An angry frown deepened three lines across his wide forehead. "What makes you suggest such stupidity?"

"I may be many things, but stupid isn't one of them."

"A lot of things?" He stood behind his desk and leaned forward, pressing his weight on his palms. "You mean like opinionated, headstrong, and impatient."

"Yes," she cried and shot her index finger into the air. "But not stupid."

The tight grip Andrew held on his temper was visible by the way his mouth was pinched until the grooves stood out tense and white. "Maybe not stupid, but incredibly inane."

Her mouth was trembling and Jo Marie knew that if she didn't get away soon, she'd cry. "Let's not argue over definitions. Stated simply, the gesture of buying me a presentable dress was not appreciated. Not in the least."

"I gathered that much, Miss Early. Now if you'll excuse me, I have a dinner engagement."

"Gladly." She pivoted and stormed across the floor ready to jerk open the office door. To her dismay, the door stuck and wouldn't open, ruining her haughty exit.

"Allow me," Andrew offered bitterly.

The damn door! It would have to ruin her proud retreat.

By the time she was in the parking lot, most of her anger had dissipated. Second thoughts crowded her mind on the drive back to the apartment. She could have at least been more gracious about it. Second thoughts quickly evolved into constant recriminations so that by the time she walked through the doorway of the apartment, Jo Marie was thoroughly miserable.

"Hi." Kelly was mixing raw hamburger for meatloaf with her hands. "Did the dress arrive?"

Kelly knew! "Dress?"

"Yes. Andrew and I went shopping for you yesterday afternoon and found the most incredibly lovely party dress. It was perfect for you."

Involuntarily, Jo Marie stiffened. "What made you think I needed a dress?"

Kelly's smile was filled with humor. "You were sewing one, weren't you? Drew said that you were really attending this function as a favor to me. And since this is such a busy time of year he didn't want you spending your nights slaving over a sewing machine.''

"Oh." A sickening feeling attacked the pit of her stomach.

"Drew can be the most thoughtful person," Kelly commented as she continued to blend the ground meat. Her attention was more on her task than on Jo Marie. "You can understand why it's so easy to love him."

A strangled sound made its way past the tightness in Jo Marie's throat.

"I'm surprised the dress hasn't arrived. Drew gave specific instructions that it was to be delivered today in case any alterations were needed."

"It did come," Jo Marie announced, more miserable than she could ever remember being.

"It did?" Excitement elevated Kelly's voice. "Why didn't you say something? Isn't it the most beautiful dress you've ever seen? You're going to be gorgeous." Kelly's enthusiasm waned as she turned around. "Jo, what's wrong? You look like you're ready to burst into tears."

"That's...that's because I am," she managed and covering her face with her hands, she sat on the edge of the sofa and wept.

Kelly's soft laugh only made everything seem worse. "I expected gratitude," Kelly said with a sigh and handed Jo Marie a tissue. "But certainly not tears. You don't cry that often."

Noisily Jo Marie blew her nose. "I...I thought I was an embarrassment...to you two...that...you didn't want me...at the party...because I didn't have...the proper clothes...and..."

"You thought what?" Kelly interrupted, a shocked, hurt look crowding her face. "I can't believe you'd even think anything so crazy."

"That's not all. I..." She swallowed. "I took the dress to...Andrew's office and practically...threw it in his face."

"Oh, Jo Marie." Kelly lowered herself onto the sofa beside her friend. "How could you?"

"I don't know. Maybe it sounds ridiculous, but I really believed that you and Andrew would be ashamed to be seen with me in an outfit I'd made myself."

"How could you come up with something so dumb? Especially since I've always complimented you on the things you've sewn."

Miserably, Jo Marie bowed her head. "I know."

"You've really done it, but good, my friend. I can just imagine Drew's reaction to your visit." At the thought Kelly's face grew tight. "Now what are you going to do?"

"Nothing. From this moment on I'll be conveniently tucked in my room when he comes for you..."

"What about the party?" Kelly's blue eyes were rounded with childlike fright and Jo Marie could only speculate whether it was feigned or real. "It's only two days away."

"I can't go, certainly you can understand that."

"But you've got to come," Kelly returned adamantly. "Mark said he'd go if you were there and I need you both. Everything will be ruined if you back out now."

"Mark's coming?" Jo Marie had a difficult time believing her brother would agree to this party idea.

She'd have thought Mark would do anything to avoid another confrontation with Andrew.

"Yes. And it wasn't easy to get him to agree."

"I can imagine," Jo Marie returned dryly.

"Jo Marie, please. Your being there means so much to me. More than you'll ever know. Do this one thing and I promise I won't ask another thing of you as long as I live."

Kelly was serious. Something about this party was terribly important to her. Jo Marie couldn't understand what. In order to attend the party she would need to apologize to Andrew. If it had been her choice she would have waited a week or two before approaching him, giving him the necessary time to cool off. As it was, she'd be forced to do it before the party while tempers continued to run hot. Damn! She should have waited until Kelly was home tonight before jumping to conclusions about the dress. Any half-wit would have known her roommate was involved.

"Well?" Kelly regarded her hopefully.

"I'll go, but first I've got to talk to Andrew and explain."

Kelly released a rush of air, obviously relieved. "Take my advice, don't explain a thing. Just tell him you're sorry."

Jo Marie brushed her dark curls from her forehead. She was in no position to argue. Kelly obviously knew Andrew far better than she. The realization produced a rush of painful regrets. "I'll go to his office first thing tomorrow morning," she said with far more conviction in her voice than what she was feeling.

"You won't regret it," Kelly breathed and squeezed Jo Marie's numb fingers. "I promise you won't."

If that was the case, Jo Marie wanted to know why she regretted it already.

To say that she slept restlessly would be an understatement. By morning, dark shadows had formed under her eyes that even cosmetics couldn't completely disguise. The silky blue dress was finished and hanging from a hook on her cloest door. Compared to the lovely creation Andrew had purchased, her simple gown looked drab. Plain. Unsophisticated. Swallowing her pride had always left a bitter aftertaste, and she didn't expect it to be any different today.

"Good luck," Kelly murmured her condolences to Jo Marie on her way out the door.

"Thanks, I'll need that and more." The knot in her stomach grew tighter every minute. Jo Marie didn't know what she was going to say or even where to begin.

Mrs. Stewart, the gray-haired guardian, was at her station when Jo Marie stepped inside Andrew's office.

"Good morning."

The secretary was too well trained to reveal any surprise.

"Would it be possible to talk to Mr. Beaumont for a few minutes?"

"Do you have an appointment?" The older woman flipped through the calendar pages.

"No," Jo Marie tightened her fists. "I'm afraid I don't."

"Mr. Beaumont will be out of the office until this afternoon."

"Oh." Discouragement nearly defeated her. "Could I make an appointment to see him then?"

The paragon of virtue studied the appointment calendar. "I'm afraid not. Mr. Beaumont has meetings scheduled all week. But if you'd like, I could give him a message."

"Yes, please," she returned and scribbled out a note that said she needed to talk to him as soon as it was convenient. Handing the note back to Mrs. Stewart, Jo Marie offered the woman a feeble smile. "Thank you."

"I'll see to it that Mr. Beaumont gets your message," the efficient woman promised.

Jo Marie didn't doubt that the woman would. What she did question was whether Andrew would respond.

By the time Jo Marie readied for bed that evening, she realized that he wouldn't. Now she'd be faced with attending the party with the tension between them so thick it would resemble an English fog.

Mark was the first one to arrive the following evening. Dressed in a pin-stripe suit and a silk tie he looked exceptionally handsome. And Jo Marie didn't mind telling him so.

"Wow." She took a step in retreat and studied him thoughtfully. "Wow," she repeated.

"I could say the same thing. You look terrific."

Self-consciously, Jo Marie smoothed out an imaginary wrinkle from the skirt of her dress. "You're sure?"

"Of course, I am. And I like your hair like that."

Automatically a hand investigated the rhinestone combs that held the bouncy curls away from her face and gave an air of sophistication to her appearance.

"When will money bags be out?" Mark's gaze drifted toward Kelly's bedroom as he took a seat.

"Any minute."

Mark stuck a finger in the collar of his shirt and ran it around his neck. "I can't believe I agreed to this fiasco."

Jo Marie couldn't believe it either. "Why did you?"

Her brother's shrug was filled with self-derision. "I don't know. It seemed to mean so much to Kelly. And to be honest, I guess I owe it to her for all the times I've teased her."

"How do you feel about Beaumont?"

Mark's eyes narrowed fractionally. "I'm trying not to feel anything."

The door opened and Kelly appeared in a red frothy creation that reminded Jo Marie of Christmas and Santa and happy elves. She had seen the dress, but on Kelly the full-length gown came to life. With a lissome grace Jo Marie envied, Kelly sauntered into the room. Mark couldn't take his eyes off her as he slowly rose to a standing position.

"Kelly." He seemed to have difficulty speaking. "You...you're lovely."

Kelly's delighted laughter was filled with pleasure. "Don't sound so shocked. You've just never seen me dressed up is all."

For a fleeting moment Jo Marie wondered if Mark had ever really seen her roommate.

The doorbell chimed and three pairs of eyes glared at the front door accusingly. Jo Marie felt her stomach tighten with nervous apprehension. For two days she'd dreaded this moment. Andrew Beaumont had arrived.

Kelly broke away from the small group and answered the door. Jo Marie watched her brother's eyes narrow as Kelly stood on her tiptoes and lightly brushed her lips across Andrew's cheek. The involuntary reaction stirred a multitude of questions in Jo Marie about Mark's attitude toward Kelly. And her own toward Andrew.

When her gaze drifted from her brother, Jo Marie discovered that Andrew had centered his attention on her.

"You look exceedingly lovely, Miss Early."

"Thank you. I'm afraid the dress I should have worn was mistakenly returned." She prayed he understood her message.

"Let's have a drink before we leave," Kelly suggested. She'd been in the kitchen earlier mixing a concoction of coconut milk, rum, pineapple and several spices.

The cool drink helped relieve some of the tightness in Jo Marie's throat. She sat beside her brother, across from Andrew. The silence in the room was interrupted only by Kelly, who seemed oblivious to the terrible tension. She chattered all the way out to the car.

Again Mark and Jo Marie were relegated to the back seat of Andrew's plush sedan. Jo Marie knew that Mark hated this, but he submitted to the suggestion without comment. Only the stiff way he held himself revealed his discontent. The party was being given by an associate of Andrew's, a builder. The minute Jo Marie heard the name of the firm she recognized it as the one that had worked on the wetlands project.

Mark cast Jo Marie a curious glance and she shook her head indicating that she wouldn't say a word. In some ways, Jo Marie felt that she was fraternizing with the enemy.

Introductions were made and a flurry of names and faces blurred themselves in her mind. Jo Marie recognized several prominent people, and spoke to a few. Mark stayed close by her side and she knew without asking that this whole party scene made him uncomfortable.

In spite of being so adamant about needing her, Kelly was now nowhere to be seen. A half hour later, Jo Marie noticed that Kelly was sitting in a chair against the wall, looking hopelessly lost. She watched amazed as Mark delivered a glass of punch to her and claimed the chair beside her roommate. Kelly brightened immediately and soon the two were smiling and chatting.

Scanning the crowded room, Jo Marie noticed that Andrew was busy talking to a group of men. The room suddenly felt stuffy. An open glass door that led to a balcony invited her outside and into the cool evening air.

Standing with her gloved hands against the railing, Jo Marie glanced up at the starlit heavens. The night was clear and the black sky was adorned with a thousand glittering stars.

"I received a message that you wanted to speak to me." The husky male voice spoke from behind her.

Jo Marie's heart leaped to her throat and she struggled not to reveal her discomfort. "Yes," she said with a relaxing breath.

Andrew joined her at the wrought-iron railing. His nearness was so overwhelming that Jo Marie closed her eyes to the powerful attraction. Her long fingers tightened their grip.

"I owe you an apology. I sincerely regret jumping to conclusions about the dress. You were only being kind."

An eternity passed before Andrew spoke. "Were you afraid I was going to demand a reward, Florence Nightingale?"

Chapter Four

Jo Marie's heart went still as she turned to Andrew with wide, astonished eyes. "You do remember." They'd spent a single, golden moment together so many months ago. Not once since Kelly had introduced Andrew as her fiancé had he given her the slightest inkling that he remembered.

"Did you imagine I could forget?" he asked quietly.

Tightly squeezing her eyes shut, Jo Marie turned back to the railing, her fingers gripping the wrought iron with a strength she didn't know she possessed.

"I came back every day for a month," he continued in a deep, troubled voice. "I thought you were a nurse."

The color ebbed from Jo Marie's face, leaving her pale. She'd looked for him, too. In all the months since the Mardi Gras she'd never stopped looking. Every time she'd left her apartment, she had silently searched through a sea of faces. Although she'd never known his name, she had included him in her thoughts every day since their meeting. He was her dream man, the stranger who had shared those enchanted moments of magic with her.

"It was Mardi Gras," she explained in a quavering voice. "I'd borrowed Kelly's uniform for a party."

Andrew stood beside her and his wintry eyes narrowed. "I should have recognized you then," he said with faint self-derision.

"Recognized me?" Jo Marie didn't understand. In the short time before they were separated, Andrew had said she reminded him of a painting he'd once seen.

"I should have known you from your picture in the newspaper. You were the girl who so strongly protested the housing development for the wetlands."

"I...I didn't know it was your company. I had no idea." A stray tendril of soft chestnut hair fell forward as she bowed her head. "But I can't apologize for demonstrating against something which I believe is very wrong."

"To thine own self be true, Jo Marie Early." He spoke without malice and when their eyes met, she discovered to her amazement that he was smiling.

Jo Marie responded with a smile of her own. "And you were there that night because of Kelly."

"I'd just left her."

"And I was on my way in." Another few minutes and they could have passed each other in the hospital corridor without ever knowing. In some ways Jo Marie wished they had. If she hadn't met Andrew that night, then she could have shared in her friend's joy at the coming marriage. As it was now, Jo Marie was forced to fight back emotions she had no right to feel.

Andrew belonged to Kelly and the diamond ring on her finger declared as much.

"And...and now you've found Kelly," she stammered, backing away. "I want to wish you both a life filled with much happiness." Afraid of what her expressive eyes would reveal, Jo Marie lowered her lashes which were dark against her pale cheek. "I should be going inside."

"Jo Marie."

He said her name so softly that for a moment she wasn't sure he'd spoken. "Yes?"

Andrew arched both brows and lightly shook his head. His finger lightly touched her smooth cheek, following the line of her delicate jaw. Briefly his gaze darkened as if this was torture in the purest sense. "Nothing. Enjoy yourself tonight." With that he turned back to the railing.

Jo Marie entered the huge reception room and mingled with those attending the lavish affair. Not once did she allow herself to look over her shoulder toward the balcony. Toward Andrew, her dream man, because he wasn't hers, would never be hers. Her mouth ached with the effort to appear happy. By the time she made it to the punch bowl her smile felt brittle and was decidedly forced. All these months she'd hoped to find the dream man because her heart couldn't forget him. And now that she had, nothing had ever been more difficult. If she didn't learn to curb the strong sensual pull she felt toward him, she could ruin his and Kelly's happiness.

Soft Christmas music filled the room as Jo Marie found a plush velvet chair against the wall and sat down, a friendly observer to the party around her. Forcing herself to relax, her toe tapped lightly against the floor with an innate rhythm. Christmas was her favorite time of year—no, she amended, Mardi Gras was. Her smile became less forced.

"You look like you're having the time of your life," Mark announced casually as he took the seat beside her.

"It is a nice party."

"So you enjoy observing the life-style of the rich and famous." The sarcastic edge to Mark's voice was less sharp than normal.

Taking a sip of punch, Jo Marie nodded. "Who wouldn't?"

"To be honest I'm surprised at how friendly everyone's been," Mark commented sheepishly. "Obviously no one suspects that you and I are two of the less privileged."

"Mark," she admonished sharply. "That's a rotten thing to say."

Her brother had the good grace to look ashamed. "To be truthful, Kelly introduced me to several of her friends and I must admit I couldn't find anything to dislike about them."

"Surprise, surprise." Jo Marie hummed the Christmas music softly to herself. "I suppose the next thing I know, you'll be playing golf with Kelly's father."

Mark snorted derisively. "Hardly."

"What have you got against the Beaumonts anyway? Kelly's a wonderful girl."

"Kelly's the exception," Mark argued and stiffened.

"But you just finished telling me that you liked several of her friends that you were introduced to tonight."

"Yes. Well, that was on short acquaintance."

Standing, Jo Marie set her empty punch glass aside. "I think you've got a problem, brother dearest."

A dark look crowded Mark's face, and his brow was furrowed with a curious frown. "You're right, I do." With an agitated movement he stood and made his way across the room.

Jo Marie mingled, talking with a few women who were planning a charity benefit after the first of the year. When they asked her opinion on an important point, Jo Marie was both surprised and pleased. Although she spent a good portion of the next hour with these older ladies, she drifted away as they moved toward the heart of the party. If Andrew had recognized her as the girl involved in the protest against the wetlands development, others might too. And she didn't want to do anything that would cause him and Kelly embarrassment.

Kelly, with her blue eyes sparkling like sapphires, rushed up to Jo Marie. "Here you are!" she exclaimed. "Drew and I have been looking for you."

"Is it time to leave?" Jo Marie was more than ready, uncomfortably aware that she could be recognized at any moment.

"No...no, we just wanted to be certain some handsome young man didn't cart you away."

"Me?" Jo Marie's soft laugh was filled with incredulity. Few men would pay much attention to her, especially since she'd gone out of her way to remain unobtrusively in the background.

"It's more of a possibility than you realize," Andrew spoke from behind her, his voice a gentle rasp against her ear. "You're very beautiful tonight."

"Don't blush, Jo Marie," Kelly teased. "You really are lovely and if you'd given anyone half a chance, they'd have told you so."

Mark joined them and murmured something to Kelly. As he did so, Andrew turned his head toward Jo Marie and spoke so that the other two couldn't hear him. "Only Florence Nightingale could be more beautiful."

A tingling sensation raced down Jo Marie's spine and she turned so their eyes could meet, surprised that he would say something like that to her with Kelly present. Silently, she pleaded with him not to make this any more difficult for her. Those enchanted moments they had shared were long past and best forgotten for both their sakes.

Jo Marie woke to the buzz of the alarm early the next morning. She sat on the side of the bed and raised her arms high above her head and yawned. The day promised to be a busy one. She was scheduled to work in the office that Saturday morning and then catch a bus to LFTF headquarters on the other side of the French Quarter. She was hoping to talk to Jim Rowden, the director and manager of the conservationists' group. Jim had asked for additional volunteers during the Christmas season. And after thoughtful consideration, Jo Marie decided to accept the challenge. Christmas was such a busy time of year that many of the other volunteers wanted time off.

The events of the previous night filled her mind. Lowering her arms, Jo Marie beat back the unexpected rush of sadness that threatened to overcome her. Andrew hadn't understood any of the things she'd tried to tell him last night. Several times she found him watching her, his look brooding and thoughtful as if she'd displeased him. No matter where she went during the course of the evening, when she looked up she found Andrew studying her. Once their eyes had met and held and everyone between them had seemed to disappear. The music had faded and it was as if only the two of them existed in the party-filled crowd. Jo Marie had lowered her gaze first, frightened and angry with them both.

Andrew and Mark had been sullen on the drive home. Mark had left the apartment almost immediately and Jo Marie had fled to the privacy of her room, unwilling to witness Andrew kissing Kelly goodnight. She couldn't have borne it.

Now, in the light of the new day, she discovered that her feelings for Andrew were growing stronger. She wanted to banish him to a special area of her life, long past. But he wouldn't allow that. It had been in his eyes last night as he studied her. Those moments at the Mardi Gras were not to be forgotten by either of them.

At least when she was at the office, she didn't have to think about Andrew or Kelly or Mark. The phone buzzed continually. And because they were short-staffed on the weekends, Jo Marie hardly had time to think about anything but airline fares, bus routes and train schedules the entire morning.

She replaced the telephone receiver after talking with the Costa Lines about booking a spring Caribbean cruise for a retired couple. Her head was bowed as she filled out the necessary forms. Jo Marie didn't hear Paula Shriver, the only other girl in the office on Saturday, move to her desk.

"Mr. Beaumont's been waiting to talk to you," Paula announced. "Lucky you," she added under her breath as Andrew took the seat beside Jo Marie's desk.

"Hello, Jo Marie."

"Andrew." Her hand clenched the ballpoint pen she was holding. "What can I do for you?"

He crossed his legs and draped an arm over the back of the chair giving the picture of a man completely at ease. "I was hoping you could give me some suggestions for an ideal honeymoon."

"Of course. What did you have in mind?" Inwardly she wanted to shout at him not to do this to her, but she forced herself to smile and look attentive.

"What would you suggest?"

She lowered her gaze. "Kelly's mentioned Hawaii several times. I know that's only place she'd enjoy visiting."

He dismissed her suggestion with a short shake of his head. "I've been there several times. I was hoping for something less touristy."

"Maybe a cruise then. There are several excellent lines operating in the Caribbean, the Mediterranean or perhaps the inside passage to Alaska along the Canadian west coast."

"No." Again he shook his head. "Where would *you* choose to go on a honeymoon?"

Jo Marie ignored his question, not wanting to answer him. "I have several brochures I can give you that could spark an idea. I'm confident that any one of these places would thrill Kelly." As she pulled out her bottom desk drawer, Jo Marie was acutely conscious of Andrew studying her. She'd tried to come across with a strict business attitude, but her defenses were crumbling.

Reluctantly, he accepted the brochures she gave him. "You didn't answer my question. Shall I ask it again?"

Slowly, Jo Marie shook her head. "I'm not sure I'd want to go anywhere," she explained simply. "Not on my honeymoon. Not when the most beautiful city in the world is at my doorstep. I'd want to spend that time alone with my husband. We could travel later." Briefly their eyes met and held for a long, breathless moment. "But I'm not Kelly, and she's the one you should consider while planning this trip."

Paula stood and turned the sign in the glass door, indicating that the office was no longer open. Andrew's gaze followed her movements. "You're closing."

Jo Marie's nod was filled with relief. She was uncomfortable with Andrew. Being this close to him was a test of her friendship to Kelly. And at this moment, Kelly was losing...they both were. "Yes. We're only open during the morning on Saturdays."

He stood and placed the pamphlets on the corner of her desk. "Then let's continue our discussion over lunch."

"Oh, no, really that isn't necessary. We'll be finished in a few minutes and Paula doesn't mind waiting."

"But I have several ideas I want to discuss with you and it could well be an hour or so."

"Perhaps you could return another day."

"Now is the more convenient time for me," he countered smoothly.

Everything within Jo Marie wanted to refuse. Surely he realized how difficult this was for her. He was well aware of her feelings and was deliberately ignoring them.

"Is it so difficult to accept anything from me, Jo Marie?" he asked softly. "Even lunch?"

"All right," she agreed ungraciously, angry with him and angrier with herself. "But only an hour. I've got things to do."

A half smile turned up one corner of his mouth. "As you wish," he said as he escorted her to his Mercedes.

Jo Marie was stiff and uncommunicative as Andrew drove through the thick traffic. He parked on a narrow street outside the French Quarter and came around to her side of the car to open the door for her.

"I have reservations at Chez Lorraine's."

"Chez Lorraine's?" Jo Marie's surprised gaze flew to him. The elegant French restaurant was one of New Orlean's most famous. The food was rumored to be exquisite, and expensive. Jo Marie had always dreamed of dining there, but never had.

"Is it as good as everyone says?" she asked, unable to disguise the excitement in her voice.

"You'll have to judge for yourself," he answered, smiling down on her.

Once inside, they were seated almost immediately and handed huge oblong menus featuring a wide variety of French cuisine. Not having sampled several of the more traditional French dishes, Jo Marie toyed with the idea of ordering the calf's sweetbread.

"What would you like?" Andrew prompted after several minutes.

"I don't know. It all sounds so good." Closing the menu she set it aside and lightly shook her head. "I think you may regret having brought me here when

I'm so hungry." She'd skipped breakfast, and discovered now that she was famished.

Andrew didn't look up from his menu. "Where you're concerned, there's very little I regret." As if he'd made a casual comment about the weather, he continued. "Have you decided?"

"Yes...yes," she managed, fighting down the dizzying effect of his words. "I think I'll try the salmon, but I don't think I should try the French pronunciation."

"Don't worry, I'll order for you."

As if by intuition, the waiter reappeared when they were ready to place their order. "The lady would like *les mouilles à la crème de saumon fumé,* and I'll have the *le canard de rouen braise.*"

With a nod of approval the red-jacketed waiter departed.

Self-consciously, Jo Marie smoothed out the linen napkin on her lap. "I'm impressed," she murmured, studying the old world French provincial decor of the room. "It's everything I thought it would be."

The meal was fabulous. After a few awkward moments Jo Marie was amazed that she could talk as freely to Andrew. She discovered he was a good listener and she enjoyed telling him about her family.

"So you were the only girl."

"It had its advantages. I play a mean game of touch football."

"I hope you'll play with me someday. I've always enjoyed a rousing game of touch football."

The fork was raised halfway to her mouth and Jo Marie paused, her heart beating double time. "I...I only play with my brothers."

Andrew chuckled. "Speaking of your family, I find it difficult to tell that you and Mark are related. Oh, I can see the family resemblance, but Mark's a serious young man. Does he ever laugh?"

Not lately, Jo Marie mused, but she didn't admit as much. "He works hard, long hours. Mark's come a long way through medical school." She hated making excuses for her brother. "He doesn't mean to be rude."

Andrew accepted the apology with a wry grin. "The chip on his shoulder's as big as a California redwood. What's he got against wealth and position?"

"I don't know," she answered honestly. "He teases Kelly unmercifully about her family. I think Kelly's money makes him feel insecure. There's no reason for it; Kelly's never done anything to give him that attitude. I never have understood it."

Pushing her clean plate aside, Jo Marie couldn't recall when she'd enjoyed a meal more—except the dinner they'd shared at K-Paul's the night Kelly and Andrew had announced their engagement. Some of the contentment faded from her eyes. Numbly, she folded her hands in her lap. Being here with Andrew, sharing this meal, laughing and talking with him wasn't right. Kelly should be the one sitting across the table from him. Jo Marie had no right to enjoy his company this way. Not when he was engaged to her best friend. Pointedly, she glanced at her watch.

"What's wrong?"

"Nothing." She shook her head slightly, avoiding his eyes, knowing his look had the ability to penetrate her soul.

"Would you care for some dessert?"

Placing her hand on her stomach, she declined with a smile. "I couldn't," she declared, but her gaze fell with regret on the large table display of delicate French pastries.

The waiter reappeared and a flurry of French flew over her head. Like everything else Andrew did, his French was flawless.

Almost immediately the waiter returned with a plate covered with samples of several desserts which he set in front of Jo Marie.

"Andrew," she objected, sighing his name, "I'll get fat."

"I saw you eyeing those goodies. Indulge. You deserve it."

"But I don't. I can't possibly eat all that."

"You can afford to put on a few pounds." His voice deepened as his gaze skimmed her lithe form.

"Are you suggesting I'm skinny?"

"My, my," he said, slowly shaking his head from side to side. "You do like to argue. Here, give me the plate. I'll be the one to indulge."

"Not on your life," she countered laughingly, and dipped her fork into the thin slice of chocolate cheesecake. After sampling three of the scrumptious desserts, Jo Marie pushed her plate aside. "Thank you, Andrew," she murmured as her fingers toyed with the starched, linen napkin. "I enjoyed the meal and...and the company, but we can't do this again." Her eyes were riveted to the tabletop.

"Jo Marie—"

"No. Let me finish," she interrupted on a rushed breath. "It...it would be so easy...to hurt Kelly and I won't do that. I can't. Please, don't make this so difficult for me." With every word her voice grew weaker and shakier. It shouldn't be this hard, her heart cried, but it was. Every womanly instinct was reaching out to him until she wanted to cry with it.

"Indulge me, Jo Marie," he said tenderly. "It's my birthday and there's no one else I'd rather share it with."

No one else...his words reverberated through her mind. They were on treacherous ground and Jo Marie felt herself sinking fast.

"Happy birthday," she whispered.

"Thank you."

They stood and Andrew cupped her elbow, leading her to the street.

"Would you like me to drop you off at the apartment?" Andrew asked several minutes later as they walked toward his parked car.

"No. I'm on my way to the LFTF headquarters." She stuck both hands deep within her sweater pockets.

"Land For The Future?"

She nodded. "They need extra volunteers during the Christmas season."

His wide brow knitted with a deep frown. "As I recall, that building is in a bad part of town. Is it safe for you to—"

"Perfectly safe." She took a step in retreat. "Thank you again for lunch. I hope you have a wonderful birthday," she called just before turning and hurrying along the narrow sidewalk.

Jo Marie's pace was brisk as she kept one eye on the darkening sky. Angry gray thunderclouds were rolling in and a cloud burst was imminent. Everything looked as if it was against her. With the sky the color of Andrew's eyes, it seemed as though he was watching her every move. Fleetingly she wondered if she'd ever escape him...and worse, if she'd ever want to.

The LFTF headquarters were near the docks. Andrew's apprehensions were well founded. This was a high crime area. Jo Marie planned her arrival and departure times in daylight.

"Can I help you?" The stocky man with crisp ebony hair spoke from behind the desk. There was a speculative arch to his bushy brows as he regarded her.

"Hello." She extended her hand. "I'm Jo Marie Early. You're Jim Rowden, aren't you?" Jim had recently arrived from the Boston area and was taking over the manager's position of the nonprofit organization.

Jim stepped around the large oak desk. "Yes, I remember now. You marched in the demonstration, didn't you?"

"Yes, I was there."

"One of the few who stuck it out in the rain, as I recall."

"My brother insisted that it wasn't out of any sense of purpose, but from a pure streak of stubbornness." Laughter riddled her voice. "I'm back because you mentioned needing extra volunteers this month."

"Do you type?"

"Reasonably well. I'm a travel agent."

"Don't worry I won't give you a time test."

Jo Marie laughed. "I appreciate that more than you know."

The majority of the afternoon was spent typing personal replies to letters the group had received after the demonstration in front of Rose's. In addition, the group had been spurred on by their success, and was planning other campaigns for future projects. At four-thirty, Jo Marie slipped the cover over the typewriter and placed the letters on Jim's desk for his signature.

"If you could come three times a week," Jim asked, "it would be greatly appreciated."

She left forty minutes later feeling assured that she was doing the right thing by offering her time. Lending a hand at Christmas seemed such a small thing to do. Admittedly, her motives weren't pure. If she could keep herself occupied, she wouldn't have to deal with her feelings for Andrew.

A lot of her major Christmas shopping was completed, but on her way to the bus stop, Jo Marie stopped in at a used-book store. Although she fought it all afternoon, her thoughts had been continually on Andrew. Today was his special day and she desperately wanted to give him something that would relay her feelings. Her heart was filled with gratitude. Without him, she may never have known that sometimes dreams can come true and that fairy tales aren't always for the young.

She found the book she was seeking. A large leather-bound volume of the history of New Orleans. Few cities had a more romantic background. Included in the book were hundreds of rare photographs of the city's architecture, courtyards, patios, ironwork and cemeteries. He'd love the book as much as she. Jo Marie had come by for weeks, paying a little bit each pay day. Not only was this book rare, but extremely expensive. Because the proprietor knew Jo Marie, he had made special arrangements for her to have this volume. But Jo Marie couldn't think of anything else Andrew would cherish more. She wrote out a check for the balance and realized that she would probably be short on cash by the end of the month, but that seemed a small sacrifice.

Clenching the book to her breast, Jo Marie hurried home. She had not right to be giving Andrew gifts, but this was more for her sake than his. It was her thank you for all that he'd given her.

The torrential downpour assaulted the pavement just as Jo Marie stepped off the bus. Breathlessly, while holding the paper-wrapped leather volume to her stomach, she ran to the apartment and inserted her key into the dead bolt. Once again she had barely escaped a thorough drenching.

Hanging her Irish knit cardigan in the hall closet, Jo Marie kicked off her shoes and slid her feet into fuzzy, worn slippers.

Kelly should arrive any minute and Jo Marie rehearsed what she was going to say to Kelly. She had to have some kind of explanation to be giving her friend's fiancé a birthday present. Her thoughts came back empty as she paced the floor, wringing her hands. It was important that Kelly understand, but finding a plausible reason without revealing herself was difficult. Jo Marie didn't want any ill feelings between them.

When her roommate hadn't returned from the hospital by six, Jo Marie made herself a light meal and turned on the evening news. Kelly usually phoned if she was going to be late. Not having heard from her friend caused Jo Marie to wonder. Maybe Andrew had picked her up after work and had taken her out to dinner. It was, after all, his birthday; celebrating with his fiancé would only be natural. Unbidden, a surge of resentment rose within her and caused a lump of painful hoarseness to tighten her throat. Mentally she gave herself a hard shake. *Stop it,* her mind shouted. *You have no right to feel these things. Andrew belongs to Kelly, not you.*

A mixture of pain and confusion moved across her smooth brow when the doorbell chimed. It was probably Mark, but for the first time in recent memory, Jo Marie wasn't up to a sparring match with her older brother. Tonight she wanted to be left to her own thoughts.

But it wasn't Mark.

"Andrew." Quickly she lowered her gaze, praying he couldn't read her startled expression.

"Is Kelly ready?" he asked as he stepped inside the entryway. "We're having dinner with my mother."

"She isn't home from work yet. If you'd like I could call the hospital and see what's holding her up." So they were going out tonight. Jo Marie successfully managed to rein in her feelings of jealousy, having dealt with them earlier.

"No need, I'm early. If you don't mind, I'll just wait."

"Please, sit down." Self-consciously she gestured toward the love seat. "I'm sure Kelly will be here any minute."

Impeccably dressed in a charcoal-gray suit that emphasized the width of his muscular shoulders, Andrew took a seat.

With her hands linked in front of her, Jo Marie fought for control of her hammering heart. "Would you like a cup of coffee?"

"Please."

Relieved to be out of the living room, Jo Marie hurried into the kitchen and brought down a cup and saucer. Spending part of the afternoon with Andrew was difficult enough. But being alone in the apartment with him was impossible. The tension between them was unbearable as it was. But to be separated by only a thin wall was much worse. She yearned to touch him. To hold him in her arms. To feel again, just this once, his mouth over hers. She had to know if what had happened all those months ago was real.

"Jo Marie," Andrew spoke softly from behind her.

Her pounding heart leaped to her throat. Had he read her thoughts and come to her? Her fingers dug unmercifully into the kitchen counter top. Nothing would induce her to turn around.

"What's this?" he questioned softly.

A glance over her shoulder revealed Andrew holding the book she'd purchased earlier. Her hand shook as she poured the coffee. "It's a book about the early history of New Orleans. I found it in a used-book store and..." Her voice wobbled as badly as her hand.

"There was a card on top of it that was addressed to me."

Jo Marie set the glass coffeepot down. "Yes...I knew you'd love it and I wanted you to have it as a birthday present." She stopped just before admitting that she wanted him to remember her. "I also heard on the news tonight that...that Rose's Hotel is undergoing some expensive and badly needed repairs, thanks to you." Slowly she turned, keeping her hands behind her. "I realize there isn't anything that I could ever buy for you that you couldn't purchase a hundred times over. But I thought this book might be the one thing I could give you...." She let her voice fade in midsentence.

A slow faint smile touched his mouth as he opened the card and read her inscription. "To Andrew, in appreciation for everything." Respectfully he opened the book, then laid it aside. "Everything, Jo Marie?"

"For your generosity toward the hotel, and your thoughtfulness in giving me the party dress and..."

"The Mardi Gras?" He inched his way toward her.

Jo Marie could feel the color seep up her neck and tinge her cheeks. "Yes, that too." She wouldn't deny how speical those few moments had been to her. Nor could she deny the hunger in his hard gaze as he concentrated on her lips. Amazed, Jo Marie watched as Andrew's gray eyes darkened to the shade of a stormy Arctic sea.

No pretense existed between them now, only a shared hunger that could no longer be repressed. A surge of intense longing seared through her so that when Andrew drew her into his embrace she gave a small cry and went willingly.

"Haven't you ever wondered if what we shared that night was real?" he breathed the question into her hair.

"Yes, a thousand times since, I've wondered." She gloried in the feel of his muscular body pressing against the length of hers. Freely her hands roamed his back. His index finger under her chin lifted her face and her heart soared at the look in his eyes.

"Jo Marie," he whispered achingly and his thumb leisurely caressed the full curve of her mouth.

Her soft lips trembled in anticipation. Slowly, deliberately, Andrew lowered his head as his mouth sought hers. Her eyelids drifted closed and her arms reached up and clung to him. The kiss was one of hunger and demand as his mouth feasted on hers.

The feel of him, the touch, the taste of his lips filled her senses until Jo Marie felt his muscles strain as he brought her to him, riveting her soft form to him so tightly that she could no longer breathe. Not that she cared.

Gradually the kiss mellowed and the intensity eased until he buried his face in the gentle slope of her neck. "It was real," he whispered huskily. "Oh, my sweet Florence Nightingale, it was even better than I remembered."

"I was afraid it would be." Tears burned her eyes and she gave a sad little laugh. Life was filled with ironies and finding Andrew now was the most painful.

Tenderly he reached up and wiped the moisture from her face. "I shouldn't have let this happen."

"It wasn't your fault." Jo Marie felt she had to accept part of the blame. She'd wanted him to kiss her so badly. "I...I won't let it happen again." If one of them had to be strong, then it would be her. After years of friendship with Kelly she owed her roommate her loyalty.

Reluctantly they broke apart, but his hands rested on either side of her neck as though he couldn't bear to let her go completely. "Thank you for the book," he said in a raw voice. "I'll treasure it always."

The sound of the front door opening caused Jo Marie's eyes to widen with a rush of guilt. Kelly would take one look at her and realize what had happened. Hot color blazed in her cheeks.

"Jo Marie!" Kelly's eager voice vibrated through the apartment.

Andrew stepped out of the kitchen, granting Jo Marie precious seconds to compose herself.

"Oh, heavens, you're here already, Drew. I'm sorry I'm so late. But I've got so much to tell you."

With her hand covering her mouth to smother the sound of her tears, Jo Marie leaned against the kitchen counter, suddenly needing its support.

Chapter Five

Are you all right?" Andrew stepped back into the kitchen and brushed his hand over his temples. He resembled a man driven to the end of his endurance, standing with one foot in heaven and the other in hell. His fingers were clenched at his side as if he couldn't decide if he should haul her back into his arms or leave her alone. But the tortured look in his eyes told Jo Marie how difficult it was not to hold and reassure her.

"I'm fine." Her voice was eggshell fragile. "Just leave. Please. I don't want Kelly to see me." Not like this, with tears streaming down her pale cheeks and her eyes full of confusion. Once glance at Jo Marie and the astute Kelly would know exactly what had happened.

"I'll get her out of here as soon as she changes clothes," Andrew whispered urgently, his stormy gray eyes pleading with hers. "I didn't mean for this to happen."

"I know." With an agitated brush of her hand she dismissed him. "Please, just go."

"I'll talk to you tomorrow."

"No." Dark emotion flickered across her face. She didn't want to see him. Everything about today had been wrong. She should have avoided Andrew, feeling as she did. But in some ways, Jo Marie realized that the kiss had been inevitable. Those brief magical moments at the Mardi Gras demanded an exploration of the sensation they'd shared. Both had hoped to dismiss that February night as whimsy—a result of the craziness of the season. Instead, they had discovered how real it had been. From now on, Jo Marie vowed, she would shun Andrew. Her only defense was to avoid him completely.

"I'm sorry to keep you waiting." Kelly's happy voice drifted in from the other room. "Do I look okay?"

"You're lovely as always."

Jo Marie hoped that Kelly wouldn't catch the detached note in Andrew's gruff voice.

"You'll never guess who I spent the last hour talking to."

"Perhaps you could tell me on the way to mother's?" Andrew responded dryly.

"Drew." Some of the enthusiasm drained from Kelly's happy voice. "Are you feeling ill? You're quite pale."

"I'm fine."

"Maybe we should cancel this dinner. Really, I wouldn't mind."

"There's no reason to disappoint my mother."

"Drew?" Kelly seemed hesitant.

"Are you ready?" His firm voice brooked no disagreement.

"But I wanted to talk to Jo Marie."

"You can call her after dinner," Andrew responded shortly, his voice fading as they moved toward the entryway.

The door clicked a minute later and Jo Marie's fingers loosened their death grip against the counter. Weakly, she wiped a hand over her face and eyes. Andrew and Kelly were engaged to be married. Tonight was his birthday and he was taking Kelly to dine with his family. And Jo Marie had been stealing a kiss from him in the kitchen. Self-reproach grew in her breast with every breath until she wanted to scream and lash out with it.

Maybe she could have justified her actions if Kelly hadn't been so excited and happy. Her roommate had come into the apartment bursting with enthusiasm for life, eager to see and talk to Andrew.

The evening seemed interminable and Jo Marie had a terrible time falling asleep, tossing and turning long past the time Kelly returned. Finally at the darkest part of the night, she flipped on the beside lamp and threw aside the blankets. Pouring herself a glass of milk, Jo Marie leaned against the kitchen counter and drank it with small sips, her thoughts deep and dark. She couldn't ask Kelly to forgive her for what had happened without hurting her roommate and perhaps ruining their friendship. The only person there was to confront and condemn was herself.

Once she returned to bed, Jo Marie lay on her back, her head clasped in her hands. Moon shadows fluttered against the bare walls like the flickering scenes of a silent movie.

Unhappy beyond words, Jo Marie avoided her roommate, kept busy and occupied her time with other friends. But she was never at peace and always conscious that her thoughts never strayed from Kelly and Andrew. The episode with Andrew wouldn't happen again. She had to be strong.

Jo Marie didn't see her roommate until the following Monday morning. They met in the kitchen where Jo Marie was pouring herself a small glass of grapefruit juice.

"Morning." Jo Marie's stiff smile was only slightly forced.

"Howdy, stranger. I've missed you the past couple of days."

Jo Marie's hand tightened around the juice glass as she silently prayed Kelly wouldn't ask her about Saturday night. Her roommate must have known Jo Marie was in the apartment, otherwise Andrew wouldn't have been inside.

"I've missed you," Kelly continued. "It seems we hardly have time to talk anymore. And now that you're going to be doing volunteer work for the foundation, we'll have even less time together. You're spreading yourself too thin."

"There's always something going on this time of year." A chill seemed to settle around the area of Jo Marie's heart and she avoided her friend's look.

"I know, that's why I'm looking forward to this weekend and the party for Drew's company. By the way, he suggested that both of us stay the night on Saturday."

"Spend the night?" Jo Marie repeated like a recording and inhaled a shaky breath. That was the last thing she wanted.

"It makes sense, don't you think? We can lay awake until dawn the way we used to and talk all night." A distant look came over Kelly as she buttered the hot toast and poured herself a cup of coffee. "Drew's going to have enough to worry about without dragging us back and forth. From what I understand, he goes all out for his company's Christmas party."

Hoping to hide her discomfort, Jo Marie rinsed out her glass and deposited it in the dishwasher, but a gnawing sensation attacked the pit of her stomach. Although she'd promised Kelly she would attend the lavish affair, she had to find a way of excusing herself without arousing suspicion. "I've been thinking about Andrew's party and honestly feel I shouldn't go—"

"Don't say it. You're going!" Kelly interrupted hastily. "There's no way I'd go without you. You're my best friend, Jo Marie Early, and as such I want you with me. Besides, you know how I hate these things."

"But as Drew's wife you'll be expected to attend a lot of these functions. I won't always be around."

A secret smile stole over her friend's pert face. "I know, that's why it's so important that you're there now."

"You didn't seem to need me Friday night."

Round blue eyes flashed Jo Marie a look of disbelief. "Are you crazy? I would have been embarrassingly uncomfortable without you."

It seemed to Jo Marie that Mark had spent nearly as much time with Kelly as she had. In fact, her brother had spent most of the evening with Kelly at his side. It was Mark whom Kelly really wanted, not her. But convincing her roommate of that was a different matter. Jo Marie doubted that Kelly had even admitted as much to herself.

"I'll think about going," Jo Marie promised. "But I can't honestly see that my being there or not would do any good."

"You've got to come," Kelly muttered, looking around unhappily. "I'd be miserable meeting and talking to all those people on my own." Silently, Kelly's bottomless blue eyes pleaded with Jo Marie. "I promise never to ask anything from you again. Say you'll come. Oh, please, Jo Marie, do this one last thing for me."

An awkward silence stretched between them and a feeling of dread settled over Jo Marie. Kelly seemed so genuinely distraught that it wasn't in Jo Marie's heart to refuse her. As Kelly had pointedly reminded her, she was Kelly's best friend. "All right, all right," she agreed reluctantly. "But I don't like it."

"You won't be sorry, I promise." A mischievous gleam lightened Kelly's features.

Jo Marie mumbled disdainfully under her breath as she moved out of the kitchen. Pausing at the closet, she took her trusted cardigan from the hanger. "Say, Kell, don't forget this is the week I'm flying to Mazatlán." Jo Marie was scheduled to take a familiarization tour of the Mexican resort town. She'd be flying with ten other travel agents from the city and staying at the Riviera Del Sol's expense. The luxury hotel was sponsoring the group in hopes of having the agents book their facilities for their clients. Jo Marie usually took the "fam" tours only once or twice a year. This one had been planned months before and she mused that it couldn't have come at a better time. Escaping from Andrew and Kelly was just the thing she needed. By the time she returned, she prayed, her life could be back to normal.

"This is the week?" Kelly stuck her head around the kitchen doorway. "Already?"

"You can still drive me to the airport, can't you?"

"Sure," Kelly answered absently. "But if I can't, Drew will."

Jo Marie's heart throbbed painfully. "No," she returned forcefully.

"He doesn't mind."

But I do, Jo Marie's heart cried as she fumbled with the buttons of her sweater. If Kelly wasn't home when it came time to leave for the airport, she would either call Mark or take a cab.

"I'm sure Drew wouldn't mind," Kelly repeated.

"I'll be late tonight," she answered, ignoring her friend's offer. She couldn't understand why Kelly would want her to spend time with Andrew. But so many things didn't make sense lately. Without a backward glance, Jo Marie went out the front door.

Joining several others at the bus stop outside the apartment building en route to the office, Jo Marie fought down feelings of guilt. She'd honestly thought she could get out of attending the party with Kelly. But there was little to be done, short of offending her friend. These constant recriminations regarding Kelly and Andrew were disrupting her neatly ordered life, and Jo Marie hated it.

Two of the other girls were in the office by the time Jo Marie arrived.

"There's a message for you," Paula announced. "I think it was the same guy who stopped in Saturday morning. You know, I'm beginning to think you've been holding out on me. Where'd you ever meet a hunk like that?"

"He's engaged," she quipped, seeking a light tone.

Slip away for awhile…
Let Silhouette Romance draw
you into a love-filled world of
fascinating men and women…
**Take 4 novels PLUS a
MYSTERY GIFT <u>FREE</u>!**

Silhouette Books, 120 Brighton Rd., P.O. Box 5084, Clifton, NJ 07015-9956

YES! Please send me 4 Silhouette novels FREE and without obligation <u>PLUS</u> my Mystery Gift…

Unless you hear from me after I receive my 4
FREE books, please send me 6 new Silhouette
Romance novels for a free 15-day examination each
month as soon as they are published. I understand that
you will bill me a total of just $11.70, with no additional
charges of any kind. There is no minimum number of
books that I must buy, and I can cancel at any time. The
first 4 books and Mystery Gift are mine to keep.

NAME _____ (please print)

ADDRESS _____

CITY _____ STATE ____ ZIP ____

Terms and prices subject to change. Your enrollment subject to acceptance by
Silhouette Books.

SILHOUETTE ROMANCE is a registered trademark.

CBR6T5

TAKE 4 FREE SILHOUETTE ROMANCE NOVELS

Plus a Mystery Gift FREE! →

BUSINESS REPLY CARD

FIRST CLASS PERMIT NO. 194 CLIFTON, N.J.

Postage will be paid by addressee

Silhouette Books
120 Brighton Road
P.O. Box 5084
Clifton, NJ 07015-9956

NO POSTAGE
NECESSARY
IF MAILED
IN THE
UNITED STATES

"He is?" Paula rolled her office chair over to Jo Marie's desk and handed her the pink slip. "You could have fooled me. He looked on the prowl, if you want my opinion. In fact, he was eyeing you like a starving man looking at a cream puff."

"Paula!" Jo Marie tried to toss off her co-worker's observation with a forced laugh. "He's engaged to my roommate."

Paula lifted one shoulder in a half shrug and scooted the chair back to her desk. "If you say so." But both her tone and her look were disbelieving.

Jo Marie read the message, which listed Andrew's office number and asked that she call him at her earliest convenience. Crumbling up the pink slip, she tossed it in the green metal wastebasket beside her desk. She might be attending this party, but it was under duress. And as far as Andrew was concerned, she had every intention of avoiding him.

Rather than rush back to the apartment after work, Jo Marie had dinner in a small café near her office. From there she walked to the Land For The Future headquarters.

She was embarrassingly early when she arrived outside of the office door. The foundation's headquarters were on the second floor of an older brick building in a bad part of town. Jo Marie decided to arrive earlier than she'd planned rather than kill time by walking around outside. From the time she'd left the travel agency, she'd wandered around with little else to do. Her greatest fear was that Andrew would be waiting for her at the apartment. She hadn't returned his call and he'd want to know why.

Jim Rowden, the office manager and spokesman, was busy on the telephone when Jo Marie arrived.

Quietly she slipped into the chair at the desk opposite him and glanced over the letters and other notices that needed to be typed. As she pulled the cover from the top of the typewriter, Jo Marie noticed a shadowy movement from the other side of the milky white glass inset of the office door.

She stood to investigate and found a dark-haired man with a worn felt hat that fit loosely on top of his head. His clothes were ragged and the faint odor of cheap wine permeated the air. He was curling up in the doorway of an office nearest theirs.

His eyes met hers briefly and he tugged his thin sweater around his shoulders. "Are you going to throw me out of here?" The words were issued in subtle challenge.

Jo Marie teetered with indecision. If she did tell him to leave he'd either spend the night shivering in the cold or find another open building. On the other hand if she were to give him money, she was confident it wouldn't be a bed he'd spend it on.

"Well?" he challenged again.

"I won't say anything," she answered finally. "Just go down to the end of the hall so no one else will find you."

He gave her a look of mild surprise, stood and gathered his coat before turning and ambling down the long hall in an uneven gait. Jo Marie waited until he was curled up in another doorway. It was difficult to see that he was there without looking for him. A soft smile of satisfaction stole across her face as she closed the door and returned to her desk.

Jim replaced the receiver and smiled a welcome at Jo Marie. "How'd you like to attend a lecture with me tonight?"

"I'd like it fine," she agreed eagerly.

Jim's lecture was to a group of concerned city businessmen. He relayed the facts about the dangers of thoughtless and haphazard land development. He presented his case in a simple, straightforward fashion without emotionalism or sensationalism. In addition, he confidently answered their questions, defining the difference between building for the future and preserving a link with the past. Jo Marie was impressed and from the looks on the faces of his audience, the businessmen had been equally affected.

"I'll walk you to the bus stop," Jim told her hours later after they'd returned from the meeting. "I don't like the idea of you waiting at the bus stop alone. I'll go with you."

Jo Marie hadn't been that thrilled with the prospect herself. "Thanks, I'd appreciate that."

Jim's hand cupped her elbow as they leisurely strolled down the narrow street, chatting as they went. Jim's voice was drawling and smooth and Jo Marie mused that she could listen to him all night. The lamplight illuminated little in the descending fog and would have created an eerie feeling if Jim hadn't been at her side. But walking with him, she barely noticed the weather and instead found herself laughing at his subtle humor.

"How'd you ever get into this business?" she queried. Jim Rowden was an intelligent, warm human being who would be a success in any field he chose to pursue. He could be making twice and three times the money in the business world that he collected from the foundation.

At first introduction, Jim wasn't the kind of man who would bowl women over with his striking good looks or his suave manners. But he was a rare, dedicated man of conscience. Jo Marie had never known anyone like him and admired him greatly.

"I'm fairly new with the foundation," he admitted, "and it certainly wasn't what I'd been expecting to do with my life, especially since I struggled through college for a degree in biology. Afterward I went to work for the state, but this job gives me the opportunity to work first hand with saving some of the—well, you heard my speech."

"Yes, I did, and it was wonderful."

"You're good for my ego, Jo Marie. I hope you'll stick around."

Jo Marie's eyes glanced up the street, wondering how long they'd have to wait for a bus. She didn't want their discussion to end. As she did, a flash of midnight blue captured her attention and her heart dropped to her knees as the Mercedes pulled to a stop alongside the curb in front of them.

Andrew practically leaped from the driver's side. "Just what do you think you're doing?" The harsh anger in his voice shocked her.

"I beg your pardon?" Jim answered on Jo Marie's behalf, taking a step forward.

Andrew ignored Jim, his eyes cold and piercing as he glanced over her. "I've spent the good part of an hour looking for you."

"Why?" Jo Marie demanded, tilting her chin in an act of defiance. "What business is it of yours where I am or who I'm with?"

"I'm making it my business."

"Is there a problem here, Jo Marie?" Jim questioned as he stepped forward.

"None whatsoever," she responded dryly and crossed her arms in front of her.

"Kelly's worried sick," Andrew hissed. "Now I suggest you get in the car and let me take you home before...." He let the rest of what he was saying die. He paused for several tense moments and exhaled a sharp breath. "I apologize, I had no right to come at you like that." He closed the car door and moved around the front of the Mercedes. "I'm Andrew Beaumont," he introduced himself and extended his hand to Jim.

"From Delta Development?" Jim's eyes widened appreciatively. "Jim Rowden. I've been wanting to meet you so that I could thank you personally for what you did for Rose's Hotel."

"I'm pleased I could help."

When Andrew decided to put on the charm it was like falling into a jar of pure honey, Jo Marie thought. She didn't know of a man, woman or child who couldn't be swayed by his beguiling showmanship. Having been under his spell in the past made it all the more recognizable now. But somehow, she realized, this was different. Andrew hadn't been acting the night of the Mardi Gras, she was convinced of that.

"Jo Marie was late coming home and luckily I remembered her saying something about volunteering for the foundation. Kelly asked that I come and get her. We were understandably worried about her taking the bus alone at this time of night."

"I'll admit I was a bit concerned myself," Jim returned, taking a step closer to Jo Marie. "That's why I'm here."

As Andrew opened the passenger's side of the car, Jo Marie turned her head to meet his gaze, her eyes fiery as she slid into the plush velvet seat.

"I'll see you Friday," she said to Jim.

"Enjoy Mexico," he responded and waved before turning and walking back toward the office building. A fine mist filled the evening air and Jim pulled up his collar as he hurried along the sidewalk.

Andrew didn't say a word as he turned the key in the ignition, checked the rearview mirror and pulled back onto the street.

"You didn't return my call." He stopped at a red light and the full force of his magnetic gray eyes was turned on her.

"No," she answered in a whisper, struggling not to reveal how easily he could affect her.

"Can't you see how important it is that we talk?"

"No." She wanted to shout the word. When their eyes met, Jo Marie was startled to find that only a few inches separated them. Andrew's look was centered on her mouth and with a determined effort she averted her gaze and stared out the side window. "I don't want to talk to you." Her fingers fumbled with the clasp of her purse in nervous agitation. "There's nothing more we can say." She hated the husky emotion-filled way her voice sounded.

"Jo Marie." He said her name so softly that she wasn't entirely sure he'd spoken.

She turned back to him, knowing she should pull away from the hypnotic darkness of his eyes, but doing so was impossible.

"You'll come to my party?"

She wanted to explain her decision to attend—she hadn't wanted to go—but one glance at Andrew said that he understood. Words were unnecessary.

"It's going to be difficult for us both for a while."

He seemed to imply things would grow easier with time. Jo Marie sincerely doubted that they ever would.

"You'll come?" he prompted softly.

Slowly she nodded. Jo Marie hadn't realized how tense she was until she exhaled and felt some of the coiled tightness leave her body. "Yes, I'll...be at the party." Her breathy stammer spoke volumes.

"And wear the dress I gave you?"

She ended up nodding again, her tongue unable to form words.

"I've dreamed of you walking into my arms wearing that dress," he added on a husky tremor, then shook his head as if he regretted having spoken.

Being alone with him in the close confines of the car was torture. Her once restless fingers lay limp in her lap. Jo Marie didn't know how she was going to avoid Andrew when Kelly seemed to be constantly throwing them together. But she must for her own peace of mind...she must.

All too quickly the brief respite of her trip to Mazatlán was over. Saturday arrived and Kelly and Jo Marie were brought to Andrew's home, which was a faithful reproduction of an antebellum mansion.

The dress he'd purchased was hanging in the closet of the bedroom she was to share with Kelly. Her friend threw herself across the canopy bed and exhaled on a happy sigh.

"Isn't this place something?"

Jo Marie didn't answer for a moment, her gaze falling on the dress that hung alone in the closet. "It's magnificent." There was little else that would describe this palace. The house was a three-story structure with huge white pillars and dark shutters. It faced the Mississippi River and had a huge garden in the back. Jo Marie learned that it was his mother who took an avid interest in the wide variety of flowers that grew in abundance there.

The rooms were large, their walls adorned with paintings and works of art. If Jo Marie was ever to doubt Andrew's wealth and position, his home would prove to be a constant reminder.

"Drew built it himself," Kelly explained with a proud lilt to her voice. "I don't mean he pounded in every nail, but he was here every day while it was being constructed. It took months."

"I can imagine." And no expense had been spared from the look of things.

"I suppose we should think about getting ready," Kelly continued. "I don't mind telling you that I've had a queasy stomach all day dreading this thing."

Kelly had! Jo Marie nearly laughed aloud. This party had haunted her all week. Even Mazatlán hadn't been far enough away to dispel the feeling of dread.

Jo Marie could hear the music drifting in from the reception hall by the time she had put on the finishing touches of her makeup. Kelly had already joined Andrew. A quick survey in the full-length mirror assured her that the beautiful gown was the most elegant thing she would ever own. The reflection that came back to her of a tall, regal woman was barely recognizable as herself. The dark crown of curls was styled on top of her head with a few stray tendrils curling about her ears. A lone strand of pearls graced her neck.

Self-consciously she moved from the room, closing the door. From the top of the winding stairway, she looked down on a milling crowd of arriving guests. Holding in her breath, she placed her gloved hand on the polished bannister, exhaled, and made her descent. Keeping her eyes on her feet for fear of tripping, Jo Marie was surprised when she glanced down to find Andrew waiting for her at the bottom of the staircase.

As he gave her his hand, their eyes met and held in a tender exchange. "You're beautiful."

The deep husky tone in his voice took her breath away and Jo Marie could do nothing more than smile in return.

Taking her hand, Andrew tucked it securely in the crook of his elbow and led her into the room where the other guests were mingling. Everyone was meeting for drinks in the huge living room and once the party was complete they would be moving up to the ballroom on the third floor. The evening was to culminate in a midnight buffet.

With Andrew holding her close by his side, Jo Marie had little option but to follow where he led. Moving from one end of the room to the other, he introduced her to so many people that her head swam trying to remember their names. Fortunately, Kelly and Andrew's engagement hadn't been officially announced and Jo Marie wasn't forced to make repeated explanations. Nonetheless, she was uncomfortable with the way he was linking the two of them together.

"Where's Kelly?" Jo Marie asked under her breath. "She should be the one with you. Not me."

"Kelly's with Mark on the other side of the room."

Jo Marie faltered in midstep and Andrew's hold tightened as he dropped his arm and slipped it around her slim waist. "With Mark?" She couldn't imagine her brother attending this party. Not feeling the way he did about Andrew.

Not until they were upstairs and the music was playing did Jo Marie have an opportunity to talk to her brother. He was sitting against the wall in a high-backed mahogany chair with a velvet cushion. Kelly was at his side. Jo Marie couldn't recall a time she'd seen her brother dress so formally or look more handsome. He'd had his hair trimmed and was clean shaven. She'd never dreamed she'd see Mark in a tuxedo.

"Hello, Mark."

Her brother looked up, guilt etched on his face. "Jo Marie." Briefly he exchanged looks with Kelly and stood, offering Jo Marie his seat.

"Thanks," she said as she sat and slipped the high-heeled sandals from her toes. "My feet could use a few moments' rest."

"You certainly haven't lacked for partners," Kelly observed happily. "You're a hit, Jo Marie. Even Mark was saying he couldn't believe you were his sister."

"I've never seen you look more attractive," Mark added. "But then I bet you didn't buy that dress out of petty cash either."

If there was a note of censure in her brother's voice, Jo Marie didn't hear it. "No." Absently her hand smoothed the silk skirt. "It was a gift from Andrew...and Kelly." Hastily she added her roommate's name. "I must admit though, I'm surprised to see you here."

"Andrew extended the invitation personally," Mark replied, holding his back ramrod stiff as he stared straight ahead.

Not understanding, Jo Marie glanced at her roommate. "Mark came for me," Kelly explained, her voice soft and vulnerable. "Because I...because I wanted him here."

"We're both here for you, Kelly," Jo Marie reminded her and punctuated her comment by arching her brows.

"I know, and I love you both for it."

"Would you care to dance?" Mark held out his hand to Kelly, taking her into his arms when they reached the boundary of the dance floor as if he never wanted to let her go.

Confused, Jo Marie watched their progress. Kelly was engaged to be married to Andrew, yet she was gazing into Mark's eyes as if he were her knight in shining armor who had come to slay dragons on her behalf. When she'd come upon them, they'd acted as if she had intruded on their very private party.

Jo Marie saw Andrew approach her, his brows lowered as if something had displeased him. His strides were quick and decisive as he wove his way through the throng of guests.

"I've been looking for you. In fact, I was beginning to wonder if I'd ever get a chance to dance with you." The pitch of his voice suggested that she'd been deliberately avoiding him. And she had.

Jo Marie couldn't bring herself to meet his gaze, afraid of what he could read in her eyes. All night she'd been pretending it was Andrew who was holding her and yet she'd known she wouldn't be satisfied until he did.

"I believe this dance is mine," he said, presenting her with his hand.

Peering up at him, a smile came and she paused to slip the strap of her high heel over her ankle before standing.

Once on the dance floor, his arms tightened around her waist, bringing her so close that there wasn't a hair's space between them. He held her securely as if challenging her to move. Jo Marie discovered that she couldn't. This inexplicable feeling was beyond argument. With her hands resting on his muscular shoulders, she leaned her head against his broad chest and sighed her contentment.

She spoke first. "It's a wonderful party."

"You're more comfortable now, aren't you?" His fingers moved up and down her back in a leisurely exercise, drugging her with his firm caress against her bare skin.

"What do you mean?" She wasn't sure she understood his question and slowly lifted her gaze.

"Last week, you stayed on the outskirts of the crowd afraid of joining in or being yourself."

"Last week I was terrified that someone would recognize me as the one who had once demonstrated against you. I didn't want to do anything that would embarrass you," she explained dryly. Her cheek was pressed against his starched shirt and she thrilled to the uneven thump of his heart.

"And this week?"

"Tonight anyone who looked at us would know that we've long since resolved our differences."

She sensed more than felt Andrew's soft touch. The moment was quickly becoming too intimate. Using her hands for leverage, Jo Marie straightened, creating a space between them. "Does it bother you to have my brother dance with Kelly?"

Andrew looked back at her blankly. "No. Should it?"

"She's your fiancée." To the best of Jo Marie's knowledge, Andrew hadn't said more than a few words to Kelly all evening.

A cloud of emotion darkened his face. "She's wearing my ring."

"And...and you care for her."

Andrew's hold tightened painfully around her waist. "Yes, I care for Kelly. We've always been close." His eyes darkened to the color of burnt silver. "Perhaps too close."

The applause was polite when the dance number finished.

Jo Marie couldn't escape fast enough. She made an excuse and headed for the powder room. Andrew wasn't pleased and it showed in the grim set of his mouth, but he didn't try to stop her. Things weren't right. Mark shouldn't be sitting like an avenging angel at Kelly's side and Andrew should at least show some sign of jealousy.

When she returned to the ballroom, Andrew was busy and Jo Marie decided to sort through her thoughts in the fresh night air. A curtained glass door that led to the balcony was open, and unnoticed she slipped silently into the dark. A flash of white captured her attention and Jo Marie realized she wasn't alone. Inadvertently, she had invaded the private world of two young lovers. With their arms wrapped around each other they were locked in a passionate embrace. Smiling softly to herself, she turned to escape as silently as she'd come. But something stopped her. A sickening knot tightened her stomach.

The couple so passionately embracing were Kelly and Mark.

Chapter Six

Jo Marie woke just as dawn broke over a cloudless horizon. Standing at the bedroom window, she pressed her palms against the sill and surveyed the beauty of the landscape before her. Turning, she glanced at Kelly's sleeping figure. Her hands fell limply to her side as her face darkened with uncertainty. Last night while they'd prepared for bed, Jo Marie had been determined to confront her friend with the kiss she'd unintentionally witnessed. But when they'd turned out the lights, Kelly had chatted happily about the success of the party and what a good time she'd had. And Jo Marie had lost her nerve. What Mark and Kelly did wasn't any of her business, she mused. In addition, she had no right to judge her brother and her friend when she and Andrew had done the same thing.

The memory of Andrew's kiss produce a breathlessness, and surrendering to the feeling, Jo Marie closed her eyes. The infinitely sweet touch of his mouth seemed to have branded her. Her fingers shook as she raised them to the gentle curve of her lips. Jo Marie doubted that she would ever feel the same overpowering rush of sensation at another man's touch. Andrew was special, her dream man. Whole lifetimes could pass and she'd never find anyone she'd love more. The powerful ache in her heart drove her to the closet where a change of clothes were hanging.

Dawn's light was creeping up the stairs, awaking a sleeping world, when Jo Marie softly clicked the bedroom door closed. Her overnight bag was clenched tightly in her hand. She hated to sneak out, but the thought of facing everyone over the breakfast table was more than she could bear. Andrew and Kelly needed to be alone. Time together was something they hadn't had much of lately. This morning would be the perfect opportunity for them to sit down and discuss their coming marriage. Jo Marie would only be an intruder.

Moving so softly that no one was likely to hear her, Jo Marie crept down the stairs to the wide entry hall. She was tiptoeing toward the front door when a voice behind her interrupted her quiet departure.

"What do you think you're doing?"

Releasing a tiny, startled cry, Jo Marie dropped the suitcase and held her hand to her breast.

"Andrew, you've frightened me to death."

"Just what are you up to?"

"I'm...I'm leaving."

"That's fairly easy to ascertain. What I want to know is why." His angry gaze locked with hers, refusing to allow her to turn away.

"I thought you and Kelly should spend some time together and...and I wanted to be gone this morning before everyone woke." Regret crept into her voice. Maybe sneaking out like this wasn't such a fabulous idea, after all.

He stared at her in the dim light as if he could examine her soul with his penetrating gaze. When he spoke again, his tone was lighter. "And just how did you expect to get to town. Walk?"

"Exactly."

"But it's miles."

"All the more reason to get an early start," she reasoned.

Andrew studied her as though he couldn't believe what he was hearing. "Is running away so important that you would sneak out of here like a cat burglar and not tell anyone where you're headed?"

How quickly her plan had backfired. By trying to leave unobtrusively she'd only managed to offend Andrew when she had every reason to thank him. "I didn't mean to be rude, although I can see now that I have been. I suppose this makes me look like an ungrateful house guest."

His answer was to narrow his eyes fractionally.

"I want you to know I left a note that explained where I was going to both you and Kelly. It's on the nightstand."

"And what did you say?"

"That I enjoyed the party immensely and that I've never felt more beautiful in any dress."

A brief troubled look stole over Andrew's face. "Once," he murmured absently. "Only onece have you been more lovely." There was an unexpectedly gentle quality to his voice.

Her eyelashes fluttered closed. Andrew was reminding her of that February night. He too hadn't been able to forget the Mardi Gras. After all this time, after everything that had transpired since, neither of them could forget. The spell was as potent today as it had been those many months ago.

"Is that coffee I smell?" The question sought an invitation to linger with Andrew. Her original intent had been to escape so that Kelly could have the opportunity to spend this time alone with him. Instead, Jo Marie was seeking it herself. To sit in the early light of dawn and savor a few solitary minutes alone with Andrew was too tempting to ignore.

"Come and I'll get you a cup." Andrew led her toward the back of the house and his den. The room held a faint scent of leather and tobacco that mingled with the aroma of musk and spice.

Three walls were lined with leather-bound books that reached from the floor to the ceiling. Two wing chairs were angled in front of a large fireplace.

"Go ahead and sit down. I'll be back in a moment with the coffee."

A contented smile brightened Jo Marie's eyes as she sat and noticed the leather volume she'd given him lying open on the ottoman. Apparently he'd been reading it when he heard the noise at the front of the house and had left to investigate.

Andrew returned and carefully handed her the steaming earthenware mug. His eyes followed her gaze which rested on the open book. "I've been reading it. This is a wonderful book. Where did you ever find something like this?"

"I've known about it for a long time, but there were only a few volumes available. I located this one about three months ago in a used-book store."

"It's very special to me because of the woman who bought it for me."

"No." Jo Marie's eyes widened as she lightly tossed her head from side to side. "Don't let that be the reason. Appreciate the book for all the interesting details it gives of New Orleans' colorful past. Or admire the pictures of the city architects' skill. But don't treasure it because of me."

Andrew looked for a moment as if he wanted to argue, but she spoke again.

"When you read this book ten, maybe twenty, years from now, I'll only be someone who briefly passed through your life. I imagine you'll have trouble remembering what I looked like."

"You'll never be anyone who flits in and out of my life."

He said it with such intensity that Jo Marie's fingers tightened around the thick handle of the mug. "All right," she agreed with a shaky laugh. "I'll admit I barged into your peaceful existence long before Kelly introduced us but—"

"But," Andrew interrupted on a short laugh, "it seems we were destined to meet. Do you honestly believe that either of us will ever forget that night?" A faint smile touched his eyes as he regarded her steadily.

Jo Marie knew that she never would. Andrew was her dream man. It had been far more than mere fate that had brought them together, something almost spiritual.

"No," she answered softly. "I'll never forget."

Regret moved across his features, creasing his wide brow and pinching his mouth. "Nor will I forget," he murmured in a husky voice that sounded very much like a vow.

The air between them was electric. For months she'd thought of Andrew as the dream man. But coming to know him these past weeks had proven that he wasn't an apparition, but real. Human, vulnerable, proud, intelligent, generous—and everything that she had ever hoped to find in a man. She lowered her gaze and studied the dark depths of the steaming coffee. Andrew might be everything she had ever wanted in a man, but Kelly wore his ring and her roommate's stake on him was far more tangible than her own romantic dreams.

Taking an exaggerated drink of her coffee, Jo Marie carefully set aside the rose-colored mug and stood. "I really should be leaving."

"Please stay," Andrew requested. "Just sit with me a few minutes longer. It's been in this room that I've sat and thought about you so often. I'd always hoped that someday you would join me here."

Jo Marie dipped her head, her heart singing with the beauty of his words. She'd fantasized about him too. Since their meeting, her mind had conjured up his image so often that it wouldn't hurt to steal a few more moments of innocent happiness. Kelly would have him for a lifetime. Jo Marie had only today.

"I'll stay," she agreed and her voice throbbed with the excited beat of her heart.

"And when the times comes, I'll drive you back to the city."

She nodded her acceptance and finished her coffee. "It's so peaceful in here. It feels like all I need to do is lean my head back, close my eyes and I'll be asleep."

"Go ahead," he urged in a whispered tone.

A smile touched her radiant features. She didn't want to fall asleep and miss these precious moments alone with him. "No." She shook her head. "Tell me about yourself. I want to know everything."

His returning smile was wry. "I'd hate to bore you."

"Bore me!" Her small laugh was incredulous. "There's no chance of that."

"All right, but lay back and close your eyes and let me start by telling you that I had a good childhood with parents who deeply loved each other."

As he requested, Jo Marie rested her head against the cushion and closed her eyes. "My parents are wonderful too."

"But being raised in an ideal family has its draw-backs," Andrew continued in a low, soothing voice. "When it came time for me to think about a wife and starting a family there was always a fear in the back of my mind that I would never find the happiness my parents shared. My father wasn't an easy man to love. And I won't be either."

In her mind, Jo Marie took exception to that, but she said nothing. The room was warm, and slipping off her shoes, she tucked her nylon-covered feet under her. Andrew continued speaking, his voice droning on as she tilted her head back.

"When I reached thirty without finding a wife, I became skeptical about the women I was meeting. There were some who never saw past the dollar signs and others who were interested only in themselves. I wanted a woman who could be soft and yielding, but one who wasn't afraid to fight for what she believes, even if it meant standing up against tough opposition. I wanted someone who would share my joys and divide my worries. A woman as beautiful on the inside as any outward beauty she may possess."

"Kelly's like that." The words nearly stuck in Jo Marie's throat. Kelly was everything Andrew was describing and more. As painful as it was to admit, Jo Marie understood why Andrew had asked her roommate to marry him. In addition to her fine personal qualities, Kelly had money of her own and Andrew need never think that she was marrying him for any financial gains.

"Yes, Kelly's like that." There was a doleful timbre to his voice that caused Jo Marie to open her eyes.

Fleetingly she wondered if Andrew had seen Mark and Kelly kissing on the terrace last night. If he had created the picture of a perfect woman in his mind, then finding Kelly in Mark's arms could destroy him. No matter how uncomfortable it became, Jo Marie realized she was going to have to confront Mark about his behavior. Having thoughtfully analyzed the situation, Jo Marie believed it would be far better for her to talk to her brother. She could speak more freely with him. It may be the hardest thing she'd ever do, but after listening to Andrew, Jo Marie realized that she must talk to Mark. The happiness of too many people was at stake.

Deciding to change the subject, Jo Marie shifted her position in the supple leather chair and looked to Andrew. "Kelly told me that you built the house yourself."

Grim amusement was carved in his features. "Yes, the work began on it this spring."

"Then you've only been living in it a few months?"

"Yes. The construction on the house kept me from going insane." He held her look, revealing nothing of his thoughts.

"Going insane?" Jo Marie didn't understand.

"You see, for a short time last February, only a matter of moments really, I felt my search for the right woman was over. And in those few, scant moments I thought I had met that special someone I could love for all time."

Jo Marie's heart was pounding so fast and loud that she wondered why it didn't burst right out of her chest. The thickening in her throat made swallowing painful. Each breath became labored as she turned her face away, unable to meet Andrew's gaze.

"But after those few minutes, I lost her," Andrew continued. "Ironically, I'd searched a lifetime for that special woman, and within a matter of minutes, she was gone. God knows I tried to find her again. For a month I went back to the spot where I'd last seen her and waited. When it seemed that all was lost I discovered I couldn't get the memory of her out of my mind. I even hired a detective to find her for me. For months he checked every hospital in the city, searching for her. But you see, at the time I thought she was a nurse."

Jo Marie felt moisture gathering in the corner of her eyes. Never had she believed that Andrew had looked for her to the extent that he hired someone.

"For a time I was convinced I was going insane. This woman, whose name I didn't even know, filled my every waking moment and haunted my sleep. Building the house was something I've always wanted to do. It helped fill the time until I could find her again. Every room was constructed with her in mind."

Andrew was explaining that he'd built the house for her. Jo Marie had thought she'd be uncomfortable in such a magnificent home. But she'd immediately felt the welcome in the walls. Little had she dreamed the reason why.

"Sometimes," Jo Marie began awkwardly, "people build things up in their minds and when they're confronted with reality they're inevitably disappointed." Andrew was making her out to be wearing angel's wings. So much time had passed that he no longer saw her as flesh and bone, but a wonderful fantasy his mind had created.

"Not this time," he countered smoothly.

"I wondered where I'd find the two of you." A sleepy-eyed Kelly stood poised in the doorway of the den. There wasn't any censure in her voice, only her usual morning brightness. "Isn't it a marvelous morning? The sun's up and there's a bright new day just waiting for us."

Self-consciously, Jo Marie unwound her feet from beneath her and reached for her shoes. "What time is it?"

"A quarter to eight." Andrew supplied the information.

Jo Marie was amazed to realize that she'd spent the better part of two hours talking to him. But it would be time she'd treasure all her life.

"If you have no objections," Kelly murmured and paused to take a wide yawn, "I thought I'd go to the hospital this morning. There's a special...patient I'd like to stop in and visit."

A patient or Mark, Jo Marie wanted to ask. Her brother had mentioned last night that he was going to be on duty in the morning. Jo Marie turned to Andrew, waiting for a reaction from him. Surely he would say or do something to stop her. Kelly was his fiancée and both of them seemed to be regarding their commitment to each other lightly.

"No problem." Andrew spoke at last. "In fact I thought I'd go into the city myself this morning. It is a beautiful day and there's no better way to spend a portion of it than in the most beautiful city in the world. You don't mind if I tag along with you, do you, Jo Marie?"

Half of her wanted to cry out in exaltation. If there was anything she wished to give of herself to Andrew it was her love of New Orleans. But at the same time she wanted to shake both Andrew and Kelly for the careless attitude they had toward their relationship.

"I'd like you to come." Jo Marie spoke finally, answering Andrew.

It didn't take Kelly more than a few moments to pack her things and be ready to leave. In her rush, she'd obviously missed the two sealed envelopes Jo Marie had left propped against the lamp on Kelly's nightstand. Or if she had discovered them, Kelly chose not to mention it. Not that it mattered, Jo Marie decided as Andrew started the car. But Kelly's actions revealed what a rush she was in to see Mark. If it was Mark that she was indeed seeing. Confused emotions flooded Jo Marie's face, pinching lines around her nose and mouth. She could feel Andrew's caressing gaze as they drove toward the hospital.

"Is something troubling you?" Andrew questioned after they'd dropped Kelly off in front of Tulane Hospital. Amid protests from Jo Marie, Kelly had assured them that she would find her own way home. Standing on the sidewalk, she'd given Jo Marie a happy wave, before turning and walking toward the double glass doors that led to the lobby of the hospital.

"I think Kelly's going to see Mark," Jo Marie ventured in a short, rueful voice.

"I think she is too."

Jo Marie sat up sharply. "And that doesn't bother you?"

"Should it?" Andrew gave her a bemused look.

"Yes," she said and nodded emphatically. She would never have believed that Andrew could be so blind. "Yes, it should make you furious."

He turned and smiled briefly. "But it doesn't. Now tell me where you'd like to eat breakfast. Brennan's?"

Jo Marie felt trapped in a labyrinth in which no route made sense and from which she could see no escape. She was thoroughly confused by the actions of the three people she loved.

"I don't understand any of this," she cried in frustration. "You should be livid that Kelly and Mark are together."

A furrow of absent concentration darkened Andrew's brow as he drove. Briefly he glanced in her direction. "The time will come when you do understand," he explained cryptically.

Rubbing the side of her neck in agitation, Jo Marie studied Andrew as he drove. His answer made no sense, but little about anyone's behavior this last month had made sense. She hadn't pictured herself as being obtuse, but obviously she was.

Breakfast at Brennan's was a treat known throughout the south. The restaurant was built in the classic Vieux Carre style complete with courtyard. Because they didn't have a reservation, they were put on a waiting list and told it would be another hour before there would be a table available. Andrew eyed Jo

Marie, who nodded eagerly. For all she'd heard, the breakfast was worth the wait.

Taking her hand in his, they strolled down the quiet streets that comprised the French Quarter. Most of the stores were closed, the streets deserted.

"I was reading just this morning that the French established New Orleans in 1718. The Spanish took over the 3,000 French inhabitants in 1762, although there were so few Spaniards that barely anyone noticed until 1768. The French Quarter is like a city within a city."

Jo Marie smiled contentedly and looped her hand through his arm. "You mean to tell me that it takes a birthday present for you to know about your own fair city?"

Andrew chuckled and drew her closer by circling his arm around her shoulders. "Are you always snobbish or is this act for my benefit?"

They strolled for what seemed far longer than a mere hour, visiting Jackson Square and feeding the pigeons. Strolling back, with Andrew at her side, Jo Marie felt she would never be closer to heaven. Never would she want for anything more than today, this minute, with this man. Jo Marie felt tears mist her dusty eyes. A tremulous smile touched her mouth. Andrew was here with her. Within a short time he would be married to Kelly and she must accept that, but for now, he was hers.

The meal was everything they'd been promised. Ham, soft breads fresh from the bakery, eggs and a fabulous chicory coffee. A couple of times Jo Marie found herself glancing at Andrew. His expression revealed little and she wondered if he regretted having decided to spend this time with her. She prayed that wasn't the case.

When they stood to leave, Andrew reached for her hand and smiled down on her with shining gray eyes.

Jo Marie's heart throbbed with love. The radiant light of her happiness shone through when Andrew's arm slipped naturally around her shoulder as if branding her with his seal of protection.

"I enjoy being with you," he said and she couldn't doubt the sincerity in his voice. "You're the kind of woman who would be as much at ease at a formal ball as you would fishing from the riverside with rolled-up jeans."

"I'm not Huck Finn," she teased.

"No," he smiled, joining in her game. "Just my Florence Nightingale, the woman who has haunted me for the last nine months."

Self-consciously, Jo Marie eased the strap of her leather purse over her shoulder. "It's always been my belief that dreams have a way of fading, especially when faced with the bright light of the sun and reality."

"Normally, I'd agree with you," Andrew responded thoughtfully, "but not this time. There are moments so rare in one's life that recognizing what they are can sometimes be doubted. Of you, of that night, of us, I have no doubts."

"None?" Jo Marie barely recognized her own voice.

"None," he confirmed.

If that were so, then why did Kelly continue to wear his ring? How could he look at her with so much emotion and then ask another woman to share his life?

The ride to Jo Marie's apartment was accomplished in a companionable silence. Andrew pulled into the parking space and turned off the ignition. Jo Marie's gaze centered on the dashboard. Silently she'd hoped that he wouldn't come inside with her. The atmosphere when they were alone was volatile. And with everything that Andrew had told her this morning, Jo Marie doubted that she'd have the strength to stay out of his arms if he reached for her.

"I can see myself inside." Gallantly, she made an effort to avoid temptation.

"Nonsense," Andrew returned, and opening the car door, he removed her overnight case from the back seat.

Jo Marie opened her side and climbed out, not waiting for him to come around. A feeling of doom settled around her heart.

Her hand was steady as she inserted the key into the apartment lock, but that was the only thing that was. Her knees felt like rubber as the door swung open and she stepped inside the room, standing in the entryway. The drapes were pulled, blocking out the sunlight, making the apartment's surroundings all the more intimate.

"I have so much to thank you for," she began and nervously tugged a strand of dark hair behind her ear. "A simple thank you seems like so little." She hoped Andrew understood that she didn't want him to come any farther into the apartment.

The door clicked closed and her heart sank. "Where would you like me to put your suitcase?"

Determined not to make this situation any worse for them, Jo Marie didn't move. "Just leave it here."

A smoldering light of amused anger burned in his eyes as he set the suitcase down. "There's no help for this," he whispered as his hand slid slowly, almost unwillingly along the back of her waist. "Be angry with me later."

Any protests died the moment his mouth met hers in a demanding kiss. An immediate answering hunger seared through her veins, melting all resistance until she was molded against the solid wall of his chest. His caressing fingers explored the curve of her neck and shoulders and his mouth followed, blazing a trail that led back to her waiting lips.

Jo Marie rotated her head, giving him access to any part of her face that his hungry mouth desired. She offered no protest when his hands sought the fullness of her breast, then sighed with the way her body responded to the gentleness of his fingers. He kissed her expertly, his mobile mouth moving insistently over hers, teasing her with light, biting nips that made her yearn for more and more. Then he'd change his tactics and kiss her with a hungry demand. Lost in a mindless haze, she clung to him as the tears filled her eyes and ran unheeded down her cheeks. Everything she feared was happening. And worse, she was powerless to stop him. Her throat felt dry and scratchy and she uttered a soft sob in a effort to abate the flow of emotion.

Andrew went still. He cupped her face in his hands and examined her tear-streaked cheeks. His troubled expression swam in and out of her vision.

"Jo Marie," he whispered, his voice tortured. "Don't cry, darling, please don't cry." With an infinite tenderness he kissed away each tear and when he reached her trembling mouth, the taste of salt was on his lips. A series of long, drugging kisses only confused her more. It didn't seem possible she could want him so much and yet that it should be so wrong.

"Please." With every ounce of strength she possessed Jo Marie broke from his embrace. "I promised myself this wouldn't happen again," she whispered feeling miserable. Standing with her back to him, her hands cradled her waist to ward off a sudden chill.

Gently he pressed his hand to her shoulder and Jo Marie couldn't bring herself to brush it away. Even his touch had the power to disarm her.

"Jo Marie." His husky tone betrayed the depths of his turmoil. "Listen to me."

"No, what good would it do?" she asked on a quavering sob. "You're engaged to be married to my best friend. I can't help the way I feel about you. What I feel, what you feel, is wrong as long as Kelly's wearing your ring." With a determined effort she turned to face him, tears blurring her sad eyes. "It would be better if we didn't see each other again...at least until you're sure of what you want..or who you want."

Andrew jerked his hand through his hair. "You're right. I've got to get this mess straightened out."

"Promise me, Andrew, please promise me that you won't make an effort to see me until you know in your own mind what you want. I can't take much more of this." She wiped the moisture from her cheekbones with the tips of her fingers. "When I get up in the morning I want to look at myself in the mirror. I don't want to hate myself."

Andrew's mouth tightened with grim displeasure. He looked as if he wanted to argue. Tense moments passed before he slowly shook his head. "You deserve to be treated so much better than this. Someday, my love, you'll understand. Just trust me for now."

"I'm only asking one thing of you," she said unable to meet his gaze. "Don't touch me or make an effort to see me as long as Kelly's wearing your ring. It's not fair to any one of us." Her lashes fell to veil the hurt in her eyes. Andrew couldn't help but know that she was in love with him. She would have staked her life that her feelings were returned full measure. Fresh tears misted her eyes.

"I don't want to leave you like this."

"I'll be all right," she murmured miserably. "There's nothing that I can do. Everything rests with you, Andrew. Everything."

Dejected, he nodded and added a promise. "I'll take care of it today."

Again Jo Marie wiped the wetness from her face and forced a smile, but the effort was almost more than she could bear.

The door clicked, indicating that Andrew had gone and Jo Marie released a long sigh of pent-up emotion. Her reflection in the bathroom mirror showed that her lips were parted and trembling from the hungry possession of his mouth. Her eyes had darkened from the strength of her physical response.

Andrew had asked that she trust him and she would, with all her heart. He loved her, she was sure of it. He wouldn't have hired a detective to find her or built a huge home with her in mind if he didn't feel something strong toward her. Nor could he have held her and kissed her the way he had today without loving and needing her.

While she unpacked the small overnight bag a sense of peace came over her. Andrew would explain everything to Kelly, and she needn't worry. Kelly's interests seemed to be centered more on Mark lately, and maybe…just maybe, she wouldn't be hurt or upset and would accept that neither Andrew nor Jo Marie had planned for this to happen.

Time hung heavily on her hands and Jo Marie toyed with the idea of visiting her parents. But her mother knew her so well that she'd take one look at Jo Marie and want to know what was bothering her daughter. And today Jo Marie wasn't up to explanations.

A flip of the radio dial and Christmas music drifted into the room, surrounding her with its message of peace and love. Humming the words softly to herself, Jo Marie felt infinitely better. Everything was going to be fine, she felt confident.

A thick Sunday paper held her attention for the better part of an hour, but at the slightest noise, Jo Marie's attention wandered from the printed page and she glanced up expecting Kelly. One look at her friend would be enough to tell Jo Marie everything she needed to know.

Setting the paper aside, Jo Marie felt her nerves tingle with expectancy. She felt weighted with a terrible guilt. Kelly obviously loved Andrew enough to agree to be his wife, but she showed all the signs of falling in love with Mark. Kelly wasn't the kind of girl who would purposely hurt or lead a man on. She was too sensitive for that. And to add to the complications were Andrew and Jo Marie who had discovered each other again just when they had given up all hope. Jo Marie loved Andrew, but she wouldn't find her own happiness at her friend's expense. But Andrew was going to ask for his ring back, Jo Marie was sure of it. He'd said he'd clear things up today.

The door opened and inhaling a calming breath, Jo Marie stood.

Kelly came into the apartment, her face lowered as her gaze avoided her friend's.

"Hi," Jo Marie ventured hesitantly.

Kelly's face was red and blotchy; tears glistened in her eyes.

"Is something wrong?" Her voice faltered slightly.

"Drew and I had a fight, that's all." Kelly raised her hand to push back her hair and as she did so the engagement ring Andrew had given her sparkled in the sunlight.

Jo Marie felt the knot tighten in her stomach. Andrew had made his decision.

Chapter Seven

Somehow Jo Marie made it through the following days. She didn't see Andrew and made excuses to avoid Kelly. Her efforts consisted of trying to get through each day. Once she left the office, she often went to the LFTF headquarters, spending long hours helping Jim. Their friendship had grown. Jim helped her laugh when it would have been so easy to cry. A couple of times they had coffee together and talked. But Jim did most of the talking. This pain was so all-consuming that Jo Marie felt like a newly fallen leaf tossed at will by a fickle wind.

Jim asked her to accompany him on another speaking engagement which Jo Marie did willingly. The talk was on a stretch of wetlands Jim wanted preserved and it had been well received. Silently, Jo Marie mocked herself for not being attracted to someone as wonderful as Jim Rowden. He was everything a woman could want. In addition, she was convinced that he was interested in her. But it was Andrew who continued to fill her thoughts, Andrew who haunted her dreams, Andrew whose soft whisper she heard in the wind.

Lost in the meandering trail of her musing, Jo Marie didn't hear Jim's words as they sauntered into the empty office. Her blank look prompted him to repeat himself. "I thought it went rather well tonight, didn't you?" he asked, grinning boyishly. He brushed the hair from his forehead and pulled out the chair opposite hers.

"Yes," Jo Marie agreed with an absent shake of her head. "It did go well. You're a wonderful speaker." She could feel Jim's gaze watching her and in an effort to avoid any questions, she stood and reached for her purse. "I'd better think about getting home."

"Want some company while you walk to the bus stop?"

"I brought the car tonight." She almost wished she was taking the bus. Jim was a friendly face in a world that had taken on ragged, pain-filled edges.

Kelly had been somber and sullen all week. Half the time she looked as if she were ready to burst into tears at the slightest provocation. Until this last week, Jo Marie had always viewed her roommate as an emotionally strong woman, but recently Jo Marie wondered if she really knew Kelly. Although her friend didn't enjoy large parties, she'd never known Kelly to be intimidated by them. Lately, Kelly had been playing the role of a damsel in distress to the hilt.

Mark had stopped by the apartment only once and he'd resembled a volcano about to explode. He'd left after fifteen minutes of pacing the living-room carpet when Kelly didn't show.

And Andrew—yes, Andrew—by heaven's grace she'd been able to avoid a confrontation with him. She'd seen him only once in the last five days and the look in his eyes had seared her heart. He desperately wanted to talk to her. The tormented message was clear in his eyes, but she'd gently shaken her head, indicating that she intended to hold him to his word.

"Something's bothering you, Jo Marie. Do you want to talk about it?" Dimples edged into Jim's round face. Funny how she'd never noticed them before tonight.

Sadness touched the depths of her eyes and she gently shook her head. "Thanks, but no. Not tonight."

"Venturing a guess, I'd say it had something to do with Mr. Delta Development."

"Oh?" Clenching her purse under her arm, Jo Marie feigned ignorance. "What makes you say that?"

Jim shook his head. "A number of things." He rose and tucked both hands in his pants pockets. "Let me walk you to your car. The least I can do is see that you get safely outside."

"The weather's been exceptionally cold lately, hasn't it?"

Jim's smile was inviting as he turned the lock in the office door. "Avoiding my questions, aren't you?"

"Yes." Jo Marie couldn't see any reason to lie.

"When you're ready to talk, I'll be happy to listen." Tucking the keys in his pocket, Jim reached for Jo Marie's hand, placing it at his elbow and patting it gently.

"Thanks, I'll remember that."

"Tell me something more about you," Jo Marie queried in a blatant effort to change the subject. Briefly Jim looked at her, his expression thoughtful.

They ventured onto the sidewalk. The full moon was out, its silver rays clearing a path in the night as they strolled toward her car.

"I'm afraid I'd bore you. Most everything you already know. I've only been with the foundation a month."

"LFTF needs people like you, dedicated, passionate, caring."

"I wasn't the one who gave permission for a transient to sleep in a doorway."

Jo Marie softly sucked in her breath. "How'd you know?"

"He came back the second night looking for a handout. The guy knew a soft touch when he saw one."

"What happened?"

Jim shrugged his shoulder and Jo Marie stopped walking in mid-stride. "You gave him some money!" she declared righteously. "And you call me a soft touch."

"As a matter of fact, I didn't. We both knew what he'd spend it on."

"So what did you do?"

"Took him to dinner."

A gentle smile stole across her features at the picture that must have made. Jim dressed impeccably in his business suit and the alcoholic in tattered, ragged clothes.

"It's sad to think about." Slowly, Jo Marie shook her head.

"I got in touch with a friend of mine from a mission. He came for him afterward so that he'll have a place to sleep at least. To witness, close at hand like that, a man wasting his life is far worse to me than..." he paused and held her gaze for a long moment, looking deep into her brown eyes. Then he smiled faintly and shook his head. "Sorry, I didn't mean to get so serious."

"You weren't," Jo Marie replied, taking the car keys from her purse. "I'll be back Monday and maybe we could have a cup of coffee."

The deep blue eyes brightened perceptively. "I'd like that and listen, maybe we could have dinner one night soon."

Jo Marie nodded, revealing that she'd enjoy that as well. Jim was her friend and she doubted that her feelings would ever go beyond that, but the way she felt lately, she needed someone to lift her from the doldrums of self-pity.

The drive home was accomplished in a matter of minutes. Standing otuside her apartment building, Jo Marie heaved a steadying breath. She dreaded walking into her own home—what a sad commentary on her life! Tonight, she promised herself, she'd make an effort to clear the air between herself and Kelly. Not knowing what Andrew had said to her roommate about his feelings for her, if anything, or the details of the argument, had put Jo Marie in a precarious position. The air between Jo Marie and her best friend was like the stillness before an electrical storm. The problem was that Jo Marie didn't know what to say to Kelly or how to go about making things right.

She made a quick survey of the cars in the parking lot to assure herself that Andrew wasn't inside. Relieved, she tucked her hands inside the pockets of her cardigan and hoped to give a nonchalant appearance when she walked through the front door.

Kelly glanced up from the book she was reading when Jo Marie walked inside. The red, puffy eyes were a testimony of tears, but Kelly didn't explain and Jo Marie didn't pry.

"I hope there's something left over from dinner," she began on a forced note of cheerfulness. "I'm starved."

"I didn't fix anything," Kelly explained in an ominously quiet voice. "In fact I think I'm coming down with something. I've got a terrible stomachache."

Jo Marie had to bite her lip to keep from shouting that she knew what was wrong with the both of them. Their lives were beginning to resemble a three-ring circus. Where once Jo Marie and Kelly had been best friends, now they rarely spoke.

"What I think I'll do is take a long, leisurely bath and go to bed."

Jo Marie nodded, thinking Kelly's sudden urge for a hot soak was just an excuse to leave the room and avoid the problems that faced them.

While Kelly ran her bathwater, Jo Marie searched through the fridge looking for something appetizing. Normally this was the time of the year that she had to watch her weight. This Christmas she'd probably end up losing a few pounds.

The radio was playing a series of spirited Christmas carols and Jo Marie started humming along. She took out bread and cheese slices from the fridge. The cupboard offered a can of tomato soup.

By the time Kelly came out of the bathroom, Jo Marie had set two places at the table and was pouring hot soup into deep bowls.

"Dinner is served," she called.

Kelly surveyed the table and gave her friend a weak, trembling smile. "I appreciate the effort, but I'm really not up to eating."

Exhaling a dejected sigh, Jo Marie turned to her friend. "How long are we going to continue pretending like this? We need to talk, Kell."

"Not tonight, please, not tonight."

The doorbell rang and a stricken look came over Kelly's pale features. "I don't want to see anyone," she announced and hurried into the bedroom, leaving Jo Marie to deal with whoever was calling.

Resentment burned in her dark eyes as Jo Marie crossed the room. If it was Andrew, she would simply explain that Kelly was ill and not invite him inside.

"Merry Christmas." A tired-looking Mark greeted Jo Marie sarcastically from the other side of the door.

"Hi." Jo Marie watched him carefully. Her brother looked terrible. Tiny lines etched about his eyes revealed lack of sleep. He looked as though he was suffering from both mental and physical exhaustion.

"Is Kelly around?" He walked into the living room, sat on the sofa and leaned forward, roughly rubbing his hands across his face as if that would keep him awake.

"No, she's gone to bed. I don't think she's feeling well."

Briefly, Mark stared at the closed bedroom door and as he did, his shoulder hunched in a gesture of defeat.

"How about something to eat? You look like you haven't had a decent meal in days."

"I haven't." He moved lackadaisically to the kitchen and pulled out a chair.

Lifting the steaming bowls of soup from the counter, Jo Marie brought them to the table and sat opposite her brother.

As Mark took the soup spoon, his tired eyes held a distant, unhappy look. Kelly's eyes had revealed the same light of despair. "We had an argument," he murmured.

"You and Kell?"

"I said some terrible things to her." He braced his elbow against the table and pinched the bridge of his nose. "I don't know what made me do it. The whole time I was shouting at her I felt as if it was some stranger doing this. I know it sounds crazy but it was almost as if I were standing outside myself watching, and hating myself for what I was doing."

"Was the fight over something important?"

Defensively, Mark straightened. "Yeah, but that's between Kelly and me." He attacked the toasted cheese sandwich with a vengeance.

"You're in love with Kelly, aren't you?" Jo Marie had yet to touch her meal, more concerned about what was happening between her brother and her best friend than about her soup and sandwich.

Mark hesitated thoughtfully and a faint grimness closed off his expression. "In love with Kelly? I am?"

"You obviously care for her."

"I care for my cat, too," he returned coldly and his expression hardened. "She's got what she wants—money. Just look at who she's marrying. It isn't enough that she's wealthy in her own right. No, she sets her sights on J. Paul Getty."

Jo Marie's chin trembled in a supreme effort not to reveal her reaction to his words. "You know Kelly better than that." Averting her gaze, Jo Marie struggled to hold back the emotion that tightly constricted her throat.

"Does either one of us really know Kelly?" Mark's voice was taut as a hunter's bow. Cyncism drove deep grooved lines around his nose and mouth. "Did she tell you that she and Drew have set their wedding date?" Mark's voice dipped with contempt.

A pain seared all the way through Jo Marie's soul. "No, she didn't say." With her gaze lowered, she struggled to keep her hands from shaking.

"Apparently they're going to make it official after the first of the year. They're planning on a spring wedding."

"How...nice." Jo Marie nearly choked on the words.

"Well, all I can say is that those two deserve each other." He tossed the melted cheese sandwich back on the plate and stood. "I guess I'm not very hungry, after all."

Jo Marie rose with him and glanced at the table. Neither one of them had done more than shred their sandwiches and stir their soup. "Neither am I," she said, and swallowed at the tightness gripping her throat.

Standing in the living room, Mark stared for a second time at the closed bedroom door.

"I'll tell Kelly you were by." For a second it seemed that Mark hadn't heard.

"No," he murmured after a long moment. "Maybe it's best to leave things as they are. Good night, sis, thanks for dinner." Resembling a man carrying the weight of the world on his shoulders, Mark left.

Leaning against the front door, Jo Marie released a bitter, pain-filled sigh and turned the dead bolt. Tears burned for release. So Andrew and Kelly were going to make a public announcement of their engagement after Christmas. It shouldn't shock her. Kelly had told her from the beginning that they were. The wedding plans were already in the making. Wiping the salty dampness from her cheek, Jo Marie bit into the tender skin inside her cheek to hold back a sob.

"There's a call for you on line one," Paula called to Jo Marie from her desk.

"Thanks." With an efficiency born of years of experience, Jo Marie punched in the telephone tab and lifted the receiver to her ear. "This is Jo Marie Early, may I help you?"

"Jo Marie, this is Jim. I hope you don't mind me calling you at work."

"No problem."

"Good. Listen, you, ah, mentioned something the other night about us having coffee together and I said something about having dinner."

If she hadn't known any better, Jo Marie would have guessed that Jim was uneasy. He was a gentle man with enough sensitivity to campaign for the future. His hesitancy surprised her now. "I remember."

"How would you feel about this Wednesday?" he continued. "We could make a night of it."

Jo Marie didn't need to think it over. "I'd like that very much." After Mark's revelation, she'd realized the best thing to do was to put the past and Andrew behind her and build a new life for herself.

"Good." Jim sounded pleased. "We can go Wednesday night...or would you prefer Friday?"

"Wednesday's fine." Jo Marie doubted that she could ever feel again the deep, passionate attraction she'd experienced with Andrew, but Jim's appeal wasn't built on fantasy.

"I'll see you then. Goodbye, Jo Marie."

"Goodbye Jim, and thanks."

The mental uplifting of their short conversation was enough to see Jo Marie through a hectic afternoon. An airline lost her customer's reservations and the tickets didn't arrive in time. In addition the phone rang repeatedly.

By the time she walked into the apartment, her feet hurt and there was a nagging ache in the small of her back.

"I thought I heard you." Kelly sauntered into the kitchen and stood in the doorway dressed in a robe and slippers.

"How are you feeling?"

She lifted one shoulder in a weak shrug. "Better."

"You stayed home?" Kelly had still been in bed when Jo Marie left for work. Apparently her friend had phoned in sick.

"Yeah." She moved into the living room and sat on the sofa.

"Mark was by last night." Jo Marie mentioned the fact casually, waiting for a response from her roommate. Kelly didn't give her one. "He said that the two of you had a big fight," she continued.

"That's all we do anymore—argue."

"I don't know what he said to you, but he felt bad about it afterward."

A sad glimmer touched Kelly's eyes and her mouth formed a brittle line that Jo Marie supposed was meant to be a smile. "I know he didn't mean it. He's exhausted. I swear he's trying to work himself to death."

Now that her friend mentioned it, Jo Marie realized that she hadn't seen much of her brother lately. It used to be that he had an excuse to show up two or three times a week. Except for last night, he had been to the apartment only twice since Thanksgiving.

"I don't think he's eaten a decent meal in days," Kelly continued. "He's such a good doctor, Jo Marie, because he cares so much about his patients. Even the ones he knows he's going to lose. I'm a nurse, I've seen the way the other doctors close themselves off from any emotional involvement. But Mark's there, always giving." Her voice shook uncontrollably and she paused to bite into her lip until she regained her composure. "I wanted to talk to him the other night, and do you know where I found him? In pediatrics holding a little boy who's suffering with terminal cancer. He was rocking this child, holding him in his arms and telling him the pain wouldn't last too much longer. From the hallway, I heard Mark talk about heaven and how there wouldn't be any pain for him there. Mark's a wonderful man and wonderful doctor."

And he loves you so much it's tearing him apart, Jo Marie added silently.

"Yesterday he was frustrated and angry and he took it out on me. I'm not going to lie and say it didn't hurt. For a time I was devastated, but I'm over that now."

"But you didn't go to work today." They both knew why she'd chosen to stay home.

"No, I felt Mark and I needed a day away from each other."

"That's probably a good idea." There was so much she wanted to say to Kelly, but everything sounded so inadequate. At least they were talking, which was a major improvement over the previous five days.

The teakettle whistled sharply and Jo Marie returned to the kitchen bringing them both back a steaming cup of hot coffee.

"Thanks." Kelly's eyes brightened.

"Would you like me to talk to Mark?" Jo Marie's offer was sincere, but she wasn't exactly sure what she'd say. And in some ways it could make matters worse.

"No. We'll sort this out on our own."

The doorbell chimed and the two exchanged glances. "I'm not expecting anyone," Kelly murmured and glanced down self-consciously at her attire. "In fact I'd rather not be seen, so if you don't mind I'll vanish inside my room."

The last person Jo Marie expected to find on the other side of the door was Andrew. The welcome died in her eyes as their gazes met and clashed. Jo Marie quickly lowered hers. Her throat went dry and a rush of emotion brought a flood of color to her suddenly pale cheeks. A tense air of silence surrounded them. Andrew raised his hand as though he wanted to reach out and touch her. Instead he clenched his fist and lowered it to his side, apparently having changed his mind.

"Is Kelly ready?", he asked after a breathless moment. Jo Marie didn't move, her body blocking the front door, refusing him admittance.

She stared up at him blankly. "Ready?" she repeated.

"Yes, we're attending the opera tonight. Bizet's *Carmen*," he added as if in an afterthought.

"Oh, dear." Jo Marie's eyes widened. Kelly had obviously forgotten their date. The tickets for the elaborate opera had been sold out for weeks. Her roommate would have to go. "Come in, I'll check with Kelly."

"Andrew's here," Jo Marie announced and leaned against the wooden door inside the bedroom, her hands folded behind her.

"Drew?"

"Andrew to me, Drew to you," she responded cattily. "You have a date to see *Carmen*."

Kelly's hand flew to her forehead. "Oh, my goodness, I completely forgot."

"What are you going to do?"

"Explain, what else is there to do?" she snapped.

Jo Marie followed her friend into the living room. Andrew's gray eyes widened at the sight of Kelly dressed in her robe and slippers.

"You're ill?"

"Actually, I'm feeling better. Drew, I apologize, I completely forgot about tonight."

As Andrew glanced at his gold wristwatch, a frown marred his handsome face.

"Kelly can shower and dress in a matter of a few minutes," Jo Marie said sharply, guessing what Kelly was about to suggest.

"I couldn't possibly be ready in forty-five minutes," she denied. "There's only one thing to do. Jo Marie, you'll have to go in my place."

Andrew's level gaze crossed the width of the room to capture Jo Marie's. Little emotion was revealed in the impassive male features, but his gray eyes glinted with challenge.

"I can't." Her voice was level with hard determination.

"Why not?" Two sets of eyes studied her.

"I'm...." Her mind searched wildly for an excuse. "I'm baking cookies for the Science Club. We're meeting Saturday and this will be our last time before Christmas."

"I thought you worked Saturdays," Andrew cut in sharply.

"Every other Saturday." Calmly she met this gaze. Over the past couple of weeks, Kelly had purposely brought Jo Marie and Andrew together, but Jo Marie wouldn't fall prey to that game any longer. She'd made an agreement with him and refused to back down. As long as he was engaged to another woman she wouldn't...couldn't be with him. "I won't go," she explained in a steady voice which belied the inner turmoil that churned her stomach.

"There's plenty of time before the opening curtain if you'd care to change your mind."

Kelly tossed Jo Marie an odd look. "It looks like I'll have to go," she said with an exaggerated sigh. "I'll be as fast as I can." Kelly rushed back inside the bedroom leaving Jo Marie and Andrew separated by only a few feet.

"How have you been?" he asked, his eyes devouring her.

"Fine," she responded on a stiff note. The lie was only a little one. The width of the room stood between them, but it might as well have been whole light-years.

Bowing her head, she stared at the pattern in the carpet. When she suggested Kelly hurry and dress, she hadn't counted on being left alone with Andrew. "If you'll excuse me, I'll get started on those cookies."

To her dismay Andrew followed her into the kitchen.

"What are my chances of getting a cup of coffee?" He sounded pleased with himself, his smile was smug.

Wordlessly Jo Marie stood on her tiptoes and brought down a mug from the cupboard. She poured in the dark granules, stirred in hot water and walked past him to carry the mug into the living room. All the while her mind was screaming with him to leave her alone.

Andrew picked up the mug and followed her back into the kitchen. "I've wanted to talk to you for days."

"You agreed."

"Jo Marie, believe me, talking to Kelly isn't as easy as it seems. There are some things I'm not at liberty to explain that would resolve this whole mess."

"I'll just bet there are." The bitter taste of anger filled her mouth.

"Can't you trust me?" The words were barely audible and for an instant Jo Marie wasn't certain he'd spoken.

Everything within her yearned to reach out to him and be assured that the glorious times they'd shared had been as real for him as they'd been for her. Desperately she wanted to turn and tell him that she would trust him with her life, but not her heart. She couldn't, not when Kelly was wearing his engagement ring.

"Jo Marie." A faint pleading quality entered his voice. "I know how all this looks. At least give me a chance to explain. Have dinner with me tomorrow. I swear I won't so much as touch you. I'll leave everything up to you. Place. Time. You name it."

"No." Frantically she shook her head, her voice throbbing with the desire to do as he asked. "I can't."

"Jo Marie." He took a step toward her, then another, until he was so close his husky voice breathed against her dark hair.

Forcing herself into action, Jo Marie whirled around and backed out of the kitchen. "Don't talk to me like that. I realized last week that whatever you feel for Kelly is stronger than any love you have for me. I've tried to accept that as best I can."

Andrew's knuckles were clenched so tightly that they went white. He looked like an innocent man facing a firing squad, his eyes resigned, the line of his jaw tense, anger and disbelief etched in every rugged mark of his face.

"Just be patient, that's all I'm asking. In due time you'll understand everything."

"Will you stop?" she demanded angrily. "You're talking in puzzles and I've always hated those. All I know is that there are four people who—"

"I guess this will have to do," Kelly interrupted as she walked into the room. She had showered, dressed and dried her hair in record time.

Jo Marie swallowed the taste of jealousy as she watched the dark, troubled look dissolve from Andrew's eyes. "You look great," was all she could manage.

"We won't be too late," Kelly said on her way out.

"Don't worry," Jo Marie murmured and breathed in a sharp breath. "I won't be up; I'm exhausted."

Who was she trying to kid? Not until the key turned in the front door lock five hours later did Jo Marie so much as yawn. As much as she hated herself for being so weak, the entire time Kelly had been with Andrew, Jo Marie had been utterly miserable.

The dinner date with Jim the next evening was the only bright spot in a day that stretched out like an empty void. She dressed carefully and applied her makeup with extra care, hoping to camouflage the effects of a sleepless night.

"Don't fix dinner for me, I've got a date," was all she said to Kelly on her way out the door to the office.

As she knew it would, being with Jim was like stumbling upon an oasis in the middle of a sand-tossed desert. He made her laugh, teasing her affectionately. His humor was subtle and light and just the antidote for a broken heart. She'd known from the moment they'd met that she was going to like Jim Rowden. With him she could relax and be herself. And not once did she have to look over her shoulder.

"Are you going to tell me what's been troubling you?" he probed gently over their dessert.

"What? And cry all over my lime-chiffon pie?"

Jim's returning smile was one of understanding and encouragement. Again she noted the twin dimples that formed in his cheeks. "Whenever you're ready, I'm available to listen."

"Thanks." She shook her head, fighting back an unexpected swell of emotion. "Now what's this surprise you've been taunting me with most of the eve ning?'' she questioned, averting the subject from herself.

"It's about the wetlands we've been crusading for during the last month. Well, I talked to a state senator today and he's going to introduce a bill that would make the land into a state park." Lacing his hands together, Jim leaned toward the linen-covered table. "From everything he's heard, George claims from there it should be a piece of cake."

"Jim, that's wonderful." This was his first success and he beamed with pride over the accomplishment.

"Of course, nothing's definite yet, and I'm not even sure I should have told you, but you've heard me give two speeches on the wetlands and I wanted you to know."

"I'm honored that you did."

He acknowledged her statement with a short nod. "I should know better than to get my hopes up like this, but George—my friend—sounded so confident."

"Then you should be too. We both should."

Jim reached for her hand and squeezed it gently. "It would be very easy to share things with you, Jo Marie. You're quite a woman."

Flattery had always made her uncomfortable, but Jim sounded so sincere. It cost her a great deal of effort to simply smile and murmur her thanks.

Jim's arm rested across her shoulder as they walked back toward the office. He held open her car door for her and paused before lightly brushing his mouth over hers. The kiss was both gentle and reassuring. But it wasn't Andrew's kiss and Jim hadn't the power to evoke the same passionate response Andrew seemed to draw so easily from her.

On the ride home, Jo Marie silently berated herself for continuing to compare the two men. It was unfair to them both to even think in that mode.

The apartment was unlocked when Jo Marie let herself inside. She was hanging up her sweater-coat when she noticed Andrew. He was standing in the middle of the living room carpet, regarding her with stone cold eyes.

One glance and Jo Marie realized that she'd never seen a man look so angry.

"It's about time you got home." His eyes were flashing gray fire.

"What right is it of yours to demand what time I get in?"

"I have every right." His voice was like a whip lashing out at her. "I suppose you think you're playing a game. Every time I go out with Kelly, you'll pay me back by dating Jim?"

Stunned into speechlessness, Jo Marie felt her voice die in her throat.

"And if you insist on letting him kiss you the least you can do is look for someplace more private than the street." The white line about his mouth became more pronounced as his eyes filled with bitter contempt. "You surprise me, Jo Marie, I thought you had more class than that."

Chapter Eight

How dare you...how dare you say such things to me!'' Jo Marie's quavering voice became breathless with rage. Her eyes were dark and stormy as she turned around and jerked the front door open.

"What do you expect me to believe?" Andrew rammed his hand through his hair, ruffling the dark hair that grew at his temple.

"I expected a lot of things from you, but not that you'd follow me or spy on me. And then...then to have the audacity to confront and insult me." The fury in her faded to be replaced with a deep, emotional pain that pierced her heart.

Andrew's face was bloodless as he walked past her and out the door. As soon as he was through the portal, she slammed it closed with a sweeping arc of her hand.

Jo Marie was so furious that the room wasn't large enough to contain her anger. Her shoulders rose and sagged with her every breath. At one time Andrew had been her dream man. Quickly she was learning to separate the fantasy from the reality.

Pacing the carpet helped relieve some of the terrible tension building within her. Andrew's behavior was nothing short of odious. She should hate him for saying those kinds of things to her. Tears burned for release, but deep, concentrated breaths held them at bay. Andrew Beaumont wasn't worth the emotion. Staring sightlessly at the ceiling, her damp lashes pressed against her cheek.

The sound of the doorbell caused her to whirl around. Andrew. She'd stake a week's salary on the fact. In an act of defiance, she folded her arms across her waist and stared determinedly at the closed door. He could rot in the rain before she'd open that door.

Again the chimes rang in short, staccato raps. "Come on, Jo Marie, answer the damn door."

"No," she shouted from the other side.

"Fine, we'll carry on a conversation by shouting at each other. That should amuse your neighbors."

"Go away." Jo Marie was too upset to talk things out. Andrew had hurt her with his actions and words.

"Jo Marie." The appealing quality in his voice couldn't be ignored. "Please, open the door. All I want is to apologize."

Hating herself for being so weak, Jo Marie turned the lock and threw open the solid wood door. "You have one minute."

"I think I went a little crazy when I saw Jim kiss you," he said pacing the area in front of the door. "Jo Marie, promise me that you won't see him again. I don't think I can stand the thought of any man touching you."

"This is supposed to be an apology?" she asked sarcastically. "Get this, Mr. Beaumont," she said, fighting to keep from shouting at him as her finger punctuated the air. "You have no right to dictate anything to me."

His tight features darkened. "I can make your life miserable."

"And you think you haven't already?" she cried. "Just leave me alone. I don't need your threats. I don't want to see you again. Ever." To her horror, her voice cracked. Shaking her head, unable to talk any longer, she shut the door and clicked the lock.

Almost immediately the doorbell chimed, followed by continued knocking. Neither of them were in any mood to discuss things rationally. And perhaps it was better all the way around to simply leave things as they were. It hurt, more than Jo Marie wanted to admit, but she'd recover. She'd go on with her life and put Andrew, the dream man and all of it behind her.

Without glancing over her shoulder, she ignored the sound and moved into her bedroom.

The restaurant was crowded, the luncheon crowd filling it to capacity. With Christmas only a few days away the rush of last-minute shoppers filled the downtown area and flowed into the restaurants at lunch time.

Seeing Mark come through the doors, Jo Marie raised her hand and waved in an effort to attract her brother's attention. He looked less fatigued than the last time she'd seen him. A brief smile momentarily brightened his eyes, but faded quickly.

"I must admit this is a surprise," Jo Marie said as her brother slid into the upholstered booth opposite her. "I can't remember the last time we met for lunch."

"I can't remember either." Mark picked up the menu, decided and closed it after only a minute.

"That was quick."

"I haven't got a lot of time."

Same old Mark, always in a rush, hurrying from one place to another. "You called me, remember?" she taunted softly.

"Yeah, I remember." His gaze was focused on the paper napkin which he proceeded to fold into an intricate pattern. "This is going to sound a little crazy so promise me you won't laugh."

The edge of her mouth was already twitching. "I promise."

"I want you to attend the hospital Christmas party with me Saturday night."

"Me?"

"I don't have time to go out looking for a date and I don't think I can get out of it without offending half the staff."

In the past three weeks, Jo Marie had endured enough parties to last her a lifetime. "I guess I could go."

"Don't sound so enthusiastic."

"I'm beginning to feel the same way about parties as you do."

"I doubt that," he said forcefully and shredded the napkin in half.

The waitress came for their order and delivered steaming mugs of coffee almost immediately afterward.

Jo Marie lifted her own napkin, toying with the pressed paper edge. "Will Kelly and...Drew be there?"

"I doubt it. Why should they? There won't be any ballroom dancing or a midnight buffet. It's a pot luck. Can you picture old 'money bags' sitting on a folding chair and balancing a paper plate on her lap? No. Kelly goes more for the two-hundred-dollar-a-place-setting affairs."

Jo Marie opened her mouth to argue, but decided it would do little good. Discussing Andrew—Drew, her mind corrected—or Kelly with Mark would be pointless.

"I suppose Kelly's told you?"

"Told me what?" Jo Marie glanced up curious and half-afraid. The last time Mark had relayed any information about Drew and Kelly it had been that they were going to publicly announce their engagement.

"She's given her two-week notice."

"No," Jo Marie gasped. "She wouldn't do that. Kelly loves nursing; she's a natural." Even more surprising was the fact that Kelly hadn't said a word to Jo Marie about leaving Tulane Hospital.

"I imagine with the wedding plans and all that she's decided to take any early retirement. Who can blame her, right?"

But it sounded very much like Mark was doing exactly that. His mouth was tight and his dark eyes were filled with something akin to pain. What a mess this Christmas was turning out to be.

"Let's not talk about Kelly or Drew or anyone for the moment, okay. It's Christmas next week." She forced a bit of yuletide cheer into her voice.

"Right," Mark returned with a short sigh. "It's almost Christmas." But for all the enthusiasm in his voice he could have been discussing German measles.

Their soup and sandwiches arrived and they ate in strained silence. "Well, are you coming or not?" Mark asked, pushing his empty plate aside.

"I guess." No need to force any enthusiasm into her voice. They both felt the same way about the party.

"Thanks, sis."

"Just consider it your Christmas present."

Mark reached for the white slip the waitress had placed on their table, examining it. "And consider this lunch yours," he announced and scooted from his seat. "See you Saturday night."

"Mark said you've given the hospital your two-week notice?" Jo Marie confronted her roommate first thing that evening.

"Yes," Kelly replied lifelessly.

"I suppose the wedding will fill your time from now on."

"The wedding?" Kelly gave her an absent look. "No," she shook her head and an aura of dejected defeat hung over her, dulling her responses. "I've got my application in at a couple of other hospitals."

"So you're going to continue working after you're married."

For a moment it didn't look as if Kelly had heard her. "Kell?" Jo Marie prompted.

"I'd hoped to."

Berating herself for caring how Kelly and Andrew lived their lives, Jo Marie picked up the evening paper and pretended an interest in the front page. But if

Kelly had asked her so much as what the headline read she couldn't have answered.

Saturday night Jo Marie dressed in the blue dress that she'd sewn after Thanksgiving. It fit her well and revealed a subtle grace in her movements. Although she took extra time with her hair and cosmetics, her heart wasn't up to attending the party.

Jo Marie had casually draped a lace shawl over her shoulder when the front door opened and Kelly entered with Andrew at her side.

"You're going out," Kelly announced, stopping abruptly inside the living room. "You...you didn't say anything."

Jo Marie could feel Andrew's gaze scorching her in a slow, heated perusal, but she didn't look his way. "Yes, I'm going out; don't wait up for me."

"Drew and I have plans too."

Reaching for her evening bag, Jo Marie's mouth curved slightly upward in a poor imitation of a smile. "Have a good time."

Kelly said something more, but Jo Marie was already out the door, grateful to have escaped without another confrontation with Andrew.

Mark had given her the address of the party and asked that she meet him there. He didn't give any particular reason he couldn't pick her up. He didn't need an excuse. It was obvious he wanted to avoid Kelly.

She located the house without a problem and was greeted by loud music and a smoke-filled room. Making her way between the dancing couples, Jo Marie delivered the salad she had prepared on her brother's behalf to the kitchen. After exchanging pleasantries with the guests in the kitchen, Jo Marie went back to the main room to search for Mark.

For all the noisy commotion the party was an orderly one and Jo Marie spotted her brother almost immediately. He was sitting on the opposite side of the room talking to a group of other young men, who she assumed were fellow doctors. Making her way across the carpet, she was waylaid once by a nurse friend of Kelly's that she'd met a couple of times. They chatted for a few minutes about the weather.

"I suppose you've heard that Kelly's given her notice," Julie Frazier said with a hint of impatience. "It's a shame, if you ask me."

"I agree," Jo Marie murmured.

"Sometimes I'd like to knock those two over the head." Julie motioned toward Mark with the slight tilt of her head. "Your brother's one stubborn male."

"You don't need to tell me. I'm his sister."

"You know," Julie said and glanced down at the cold drink she was holding in her hand. "After Kelly had her tonsils out I could have sworn those two were headed for the altar. No one was more surprised than me when Kell turns up engaged to this mystery character."

"What do you mean about Kelly and Mark?" Kelly's tonsils had come out months ago during the Mardi Gras. No matter how much time passed, it wasn't likely that Jo Marie would forget that.

"Kelly was miserable—adult tonsillectomies are seldom painless—anyway, Kelly didn't want anyone around, not even her family. Mark was the only one who could get close to her. He spent hours with her, coaxing her to eat, spoon-feeding her. He even read her to sleep and then curled up in the chair beside her bed so he'd be there when she woke.''

Jo Marie stared back in open disbelief. ''Mark did that?'' All these months Mark had been in love with Kelly and he hadn't said a word. Her gaze sought him now and she groaned inwardly at her own stupidity. For months she'd been so caught up in the fantasy of those few precious moments with Andrew that she'd been blind to what was right in front of her own eyes.

''Well, speaking of our friend, look who's just arrived.''

Jo Marie's gaze turned toward the front door just as Kelly and Andrew came inside. From across the length of the room, her eyes clashed with Andrew's. She watched as the hard line of his mouth relaxed and he smiled. The effect on her was devastating; her heart somersaulted and color rushed up her neck, invading her face. These were all the emotions she had struggled against from the beginning. She hated herself for being so vulnerable when it came to this one man. She didn't want to feel any of these emotions toward him.

''Excuse me—'' Julie interrupted Jo Marie's musings ''—there's someone I wanted to see.''

''Sure.'' Mentally, Jo Marie shook herself and joined Mark, knowing she would be safe at his side.

''Did you see who just arrived?'' Jo Marie whispered in her brother's ear.

Mark's dusty dark eyes studied Kelly's arrival and Jo Marie witnessed an unconscious softening in his gaze. Kelly did look lovely tonight, and begrudgingly Jo Marie admitted that Andrew and Kelly were the most striking couple in the room. They belonged together—both were people of wealth and position. Two of a kind.

"I'm surprised that she came," Mark admitted slowly and turned his back to the pair. "But she's got as much right to be here as anyone."

"Of course she does."

One of Mark's friends appointed himself as disc jockey and put on another series of records for slow dancing. Jo Marie and Mark stood against the wall and watched as several couples began dancing on the makeshift dance floor. When Andrew turned Kelly into his arms, Jo Marie diverted her gaze to another section of the room, unable to look at them without being affected.

"You don't want to dance, do you?" Mark mumbled indifferently.

"With you?"

"No, I'd get one of my friends to do the honors. It's bad enough having to invite my sister to a party. I'm not about to dance with you, too."

Jo Marie couldn't prevent a short laugh. "You really know how to sweet talk a woman don't you, brother dearest?"

"I try," he murmured and his eyes narrowed on Kelly whose arms were draped around Andrew's neck as she whispered in his ear. "But obviously not hard enough," he finished.

Standing on the outskirts of the dancing couples made Jo Marie uncomfortable. "I think I'll see what I can do to help in the kitchen," she said as an excuse to leave.

Julie Frazier was there, placing cold cuts on a round platter with the precision of a mathematician.

"Can I help?" Jo Marie offered, looking around for something that needed to be done.

Julie turned and smiled her appreciation. "Sure. Would you put the serving spoons in the salads and set them out on the dining room table?"

"Glad to." She located the spoons in the silverware drawer and carried out a large glass bowl of potato salad. The Formica table was covered with a vinyl cloth decorated with green holly and red berries.

"And now ladies and gentleman—" the disc jockey demanded the attention of the room "—this next number is a ladies' choice."

With her back to the table, Jo Marie watched as Kelly whispered something to Andrew. To her surprise, he nodded and stepped aside as Kelly made her way to the other side of the room. Her destination was clear—Kelly was heading directly to Mark. Jo Marie's pulse fluttered wildly. If Mark said or did anything cruel to her friend, Jo Marie would never forgive him.

Her heart was in her eyes as Kelly tentatively tapped Mark on the shoulder. Engrossed in a conversation, Mark apparently wasn't aware he was being touched. Kelly tried again and Mark turned, surprise rounding his eyes when he saw her roommate.

Jo Marie was far enough to the side so that she couldn't be seen by Mark and Kelly, but close enough to hear their conversation.

"May I have this dance?" Kelly questioned, her voice firm and low.

"I thought it was the man's prerogative to ask." The edge of Mark's mouth curled up sarcastically. "And if you've noticed, I haven't asked."

"This number is ladies' choice."

Mark tensed visibly as he glared across the room, eyeing Andrew. "And what about Rockefeller over there?"

Slowly, Kelly shook her head, her inviting gaze resting on Mark. "I'm asking you. Don't turn me down, Mark, not tonight. I'll be leaving the hospital in a little while and then you'll never be bothered with me again."

Jo Marie doubted that her brother could have refused Kelly anything in that moment. Wordlessly he approached the dance floor and took Kelly in his arms. A slow ballad was playing and the soft, melodic sounds of Billy Joel filled the room. Kelly fit her body to Mark's. Her arms slid around his neck as she pressed her temple against his jaw. Mark reacted to the contact by closing his eyes and inhaling as his eyes drifted closed. His hold, which had been loose, tightened as he knotted his hands at the small of Kelly's back, arching her body closer.

For the first time that night, her brother looked completely at ease. Kelly belonged with Mark. Jo Marie had been wrong to think that Andrew and Kelly were meant for each other. They weren't, and their engagement didn't make sense.

Her eyes sought out the subject of her thoughts. Andrew was leaning against the wall only a few feet from her. His eyes locked with hers, refusing to release her. He wanted her to come to him. She couldn't. His gaze seemed to drink her in as it had the night of the Mardi Gras. She could almost feel him reaching out to her, imploring her to come, urging her to cross the room so he could take her in his arms.

With unconscious thought Jo Marie took one step forward and stopped. No. Being with Andrew would only cause her more pain. With a determined effort she lightly shook her head, effectively breaking the spell. Her heart was beating so hard that breathing was difficult. Her steps were marked with decision as she returned to the kitchen.

A sliding glass door led to a lighted patio. A need to escape for a few moments overtook her and silently she slipped past the others and escaped into the darkness of the night.

A chill ran up her arms and she rubbed her hands over her forearms in an effort to warm her blood. The stars were out in a dazzling display and Jo Marie tilted her face toward the heavens, gazing at the lovely sight.

Jo Marie stiffened as she felt more than heard someone join her. She didn't need to turn around to realize that it was Andrew.

He came and stood beside her, but he made no effort to speak, instead focusing his attention on the dark sky.

Whole eternities seemed to pass before Andrew spoke. "I came to ask your forgiveness."

All the pain of his accusation burned in her breast. "You hurt me," she said on a breathless note after a long pause.

"I know, my love, I know." Slowly he removed his suit jacket and with extraordinary concern, draped it over her shoulders, taking care not to touch her.

"I'd give anything to have those thoughtless words back. Seeing Jim take you in his arms was like waving a red flag in front of an angry bull. I lashed out at you, when it was circumstances that were at fault."

Something about the way he spoke, the emotion that coated his words, the regret that filled his voice made her feel that her heart was ready to burst right out of her breast. She didn't want to look at him, but somehow it was impossible to keep her eyes away. With an infinite tenderness, he brushed a stray curl from her cheek.

"Can you forgive me?"

"Oh, Andrew." She felt herself weakening.

"I'd go on my knees if it would help."

The tears felt locked in her throat. "No, that isn't necessary."

He relaxed as if a great burden had been lifted from his shoulders. "Thank you."

Neither moved, wanting to prolong this tender moment. When Andrew spoke it was like the whisper of a gentle breeze and she had to strain to hear him.

"When I first came out here you looked like a blue sapphire silhouetted in the moonlight. And I was thinking that if it were in my power, I'd weave golden moonbeams into your hair."

"Have you always been so poetic?"

His mouth curved upward in a slow, sensuous smile. "No." His eyes were filled with an undisguised hunger as he studied her. Ever so slowly, he raised his hand and placed it at the side of her neck.

The tender touch of his fingers against her soft skin caused a tingling sensation to race down her spine. The feeling was akin to pain. Jo Marie loved this man as she would never love again and he was promised to another woman.

"Jo Marie," he whispered and his warm breath fanned her mouth. "There's mistletoe here. Let me kiss you."

There wasn't, of course, but Jo Marie was unable to pull away. She nodded her acquiescence. "One last time." She hadn't meant to verbalize her thoughts.

He brought her into his arms and she moistened her lips anticipating the hungry exploration of his mouth over hers. But she was to be disappointed. Andrew's lips lightly moved over hers like the gentle brush of the spring sun on a hungry earth. Gradually the kiss deepened as he worked his way from one corner of her mouth to another—again like the earth long starved from summer's absence.

"I always knew it would be like this for us, Florence Nightingale," he whispered against her hair. "Even when I couldn't find you, I felt a part of myself would never be the same."

"I did too. I nearly gave up dating."

"I thought I'd go crazy. You were so close all these months and yet I couldn't find you."

"But you did." Pressing her hands against the strong cushion of his chest she created a space between them. "And now it's too late."

Andrew's eyes darkened as he seemed to struggle within himself. "Jo Marie." A thick frown marred his face.

"Shh." She pressed her fingertips against his lips. "Don't try to explain. I understand and I've accepted it. For a long time it hurt so much that I didn't think I'd be able to bear it. But I can and I will."

His hand circled her wrist and he closed his eyes before kissing the tips of her fingers. "There's so much I want to explain and can't."

"I know." With his arm holding her close, Jo Marie felt a deep sense of peace surround her. "I'd never be the kind of wife you need. Your position demands a woman with culture and class. I'm proud to be an Early and proud of my family, but I'm not right for you."

The grip on her wrist tightened. "Is that what you think?" The frustrated anger in his voice was barely suppressed. "Do you honestly believe that?"

"Yes," she answered him boldly. "I'm at peace within myself. I have no regrets. You've touched my heart and a part of me will never be the same. How can I regret having loved you? It's not within me."

He dropped her hand and turned from her, his look a mixture of angry torment. "You honestly think I should marry Kelly."

It would devastate Mark, but her brother would need to find his own peace. "Or someone like her." She removed his suit jacket from her shoulders and handed it back to him, taking care to avoid touching him. "Thank you," she whispered with a small catch to her soft voice. Unable to resist any longer, she raised her hand and traced his jaw. Very lightly, she brushed her mouth over his. "Goodbye, Andrew."

He reached out his hand in an effort to stop her, but she slipped past him. It took her only a moment to collect her shawl. Within a matter of minutes, she was out the front door and on her way back to the apartment. Mark would never miss her.

Jo Marie spent Sunday with her family, returning late that evening when she was assured Kelly was asleep. Lying in bed, studying the darkness around her, Jo Marie realized that she'd said her final goodbye to Andrew. Continuing to see him would only make it difficult for them both. Avoiding him had never succeeded, not when she yearned for every opportunity to be with him. The best solution would be to leave completely. Kelly would be moving out soon and Jo Marie couldn't afford to pay the rent on her own. The excuse would be a convenient one although Kelly was sure to recognize it for what it was.

After work Monday afternoon, before she headed for the LFTF office, Jo Marie stopped off at the hospital, hoping to talk to Mark. With luck, she might be able to convince her brother to let her move in with him. But only until she could find another apartment and another roommate.

Julie Frazier, the nurse who worked with both Kelly and Mark, was at the nurses' station on the surgical floor when Jo Marie arrived.

"Hi," she greeted cheerfully. "I don't suppose you know where Mark is?"

Julie glanced up from a chart she was reading. "He's in the doctors' lounge having a cup of coffee."

"Great. I'll talk to you later." With her shoes making clicking sounds against the polished floor, Jo Marie mused that her timing couldn't have been more perfect. Now all she needed was to find her brother in a good mood.

The doctors' lounge was at the end of the hall and was divided into two sections. The front part contained a sofa and a couple of chairs. A small kitchen area was behind that. The sound of Mark's and Kelly's voices stopped Jo Marie just inside the lounge.

"You can leave," Mark was saying in a tight, pained voice. "Believe me I have no intention of crying on your shoulder."

"I didn't come here for that," Kelly argued softly.

Jo Marie hesitated, unsure of what she should do. She didn't want to interrupt their conversation which seemed intense, nor did she wish to intentionally stay and listen in either.

"That case with the Randolph girl is still bothering you, isn't it?" Kelly demanded.

"No, I did everything I could. You know that."

"But it wasn't enough, was it?"

Jo Marie had to bite her tongue not to interrupt Kelly. It wasn't like her roommate to be unnecessarily cruel. Jo Marie vividly recalled her brother's doubts after the young child's death. It had been just before Thanksgiving and Mark had agonized that he had lost her.

"No," Mark shouted, "it wasn't enough."

"And now you're going to lose the Rickard boy." Kelly's voice softened perceptively.

Fleetingly Jo Marie wondered if this child was the one Kelly had mentioned who was dying of cancer.

"I've known that from the first." Mark's tone contained the steel edge of anger.

"Yes, but it hasn't gotten any easier, has it?"

"Listen, Kelly, I know what you're trying to do, but it isn't going to work."

"Mark," Kelly murmured his name on a sigh, "sometimes you are so blind."

"Maybe it's because I feel so inadequate. Maybe it's because I'm haunted with the fact that there might have been something more I could have done."

"But there isn't, don't you see?" Kelly's voice had softened as if her pain was Mark's. "Now won't you tell me what's really bothering you?"

"Maybe it's because I don't like the odds with Tommy. His endless struggle against pain. The deck was stacked against him from the beginning and now he hasn't got a bettor's edge. In the end, death will win."

"And you'll have lost, and every loss is a personal one."

Jo Marie didn't feel that she could eavesdrop any longer. Silently she slipped from the room.

The conversation between Mark and Kelly played back in her mind as she drove toward the office and Jim. Mark would have serious problems as a doctor unless he came to terms with these feelings. Kelly had recognized that and had set personal relationships aside to help Mark settle these doubts within himself. He'd been angry with her and would probably continue to be until he fully understood what she was doing.

Luckily Jo Marie found a parking space within sight of the office. With Christmas just a few days away the area had become more crowded and finding parking was almost impossible.

Her thoughts were heavy as she climbed from the passenger's side and locked her door. Just as she turned to look both ways before crossing the street she caught a glimpse of the dark blue Mercedes. A cold chill raced up her spine. Andrew was inside talking to Jim.

Chapter Nine

Is everything all right?" Wearily Jo Marie eyed Jim, looking for a telltale mannerism that would reveal the reason for Andrew's visit. She'd avoided bumping into him by waiting in a small antique shop across the street from the foundation. After he'd gone, she sauntered around for several additional minutes to be certain he was out of the neighborhood. Once assured it was safe, she crossed the street to the foundation's office.

"Should anything be wrong?" Jim lifted two thick brows in question.

"You tell me. I saw Andrew Beaumont's car parked outside."

"Ah, yes." Jim paused and smiled fleetingly. "And that concerns you?"

"No." She shook her head determinedly. "All right, yes!" She wasn't going to be able to fool Jim, who was an excellent judge of human nature.

A smile worked its way across his round face. "He came to meet the rest of the staff at my invitation. The LFTF Foundation is deeply indebted to your friend."

"My friend?"

Jim chuckled. "Neither one of you has been successful at hiding your feelings. Yes, my dear, sweet, Jo Marie, *your* friend."

Any argument died on her tongue.

"Would you care for a cup of coffee?" Jim asked, walking across the room and filling a Styrofoam cup for her.

Jo Marie smiled her appreciation as he handed it to her and sat on the edge of her desk, crossing his arms. "Beaumont and I had quite a discussion."

"And?" Jo Marie didn't bother to disguise her curiosity.

The phone rang before Jim could answer her. Jim reached for it and spent the next ten minutes in conversation. Jo Marie did her best to keep occupied, but her thoughts were doing a crazy tailspin. Andrew was here on business. She wouldn't believe it.

"Well?" Jo Marie questioned the minute Jim replaced the receiver.

His expression was empty for a moment. "Are we back to Beaumont again?"

"I don't mean to pry," Jo Marie said with a rueful smile, "but I'd really like to know why he was here."

Jim was just as straightforward. "Are you in love with him?"

Miserably, Jo Marie nodded. "A lot of good it's done either of us. Did he mention me?"

A wry grin twisted Jim's mouth. "Not directly, but he wanted to know my intentions."

"He didn't!" Jo Marie was aghast at such audacity.

Chuckling, Jim shook his head. "No, he came to ask me about the foundation and pick up some of our literature. He's a good man, Jo Marie."

She studied the top of the desk and typewriter keys. "I know."

"He didn't mention you directly, but I think he would have liked to. I had the feeling he was frustrated and concerned about you working here so many nights, especially in this neighborhood."

"He needn't worry, you escort me to my car or wait at the bus stop until the bus arrives."

Jim made busy work with his hands. "I had the impression that Beaumont is deeply in love with you. If anything happened to you while under my protection, he wouldn't take it lightly."

Even hours later when Jo Marie stepped into the apartment the echo of Jim's words hadn't faded. Andrew was concerned for her safety and was deeply in love with her. But it was all so useless that she refused to be comforted.

Kelly was sitting up, a blanket wrapped around her legs and torso as she paid close attention to a television Christmas special.

"Hi, how'd it go tonight?" Kelly greeted, briefly glancing from the screen.

Her roommate looked pale and slightly drawn, but Jo Marie attributed that to the conversation she'd overheard between her brother and her roommate. She wanted to ask how everything was at the hospital, but doubted that she could adequately disguise her interest.

"Tonight...oh, everything went as it usually does...fine."

"Good." Kelly's answer was absentminded, her look pinched.

"Are you feeling all right, Kell?"

Softly, she shook her head. "I've got another stomachache."

"Fever?"

"None to speak of. I think I might be coming down with the flu."

Tilting her head to one side, Jo Marie mused that Kelly had been unnaturally pale lately. But again she had attributed that to painfully tense times they'd all been through in the past few weeks.

"You know, one advantage of having a brother in the medical profession is that he's willing to make house calls."

Kelly glanced her way, then turned back to the television. "No, it's nothing to call Mark about."

But Kelly didn't sound as convincing as Jo Marie would have liked. With a shrug, she went into the kitchen and poured herself a glass of milk.

"Want one?" She raised her glass to Kelly for inspection.

"No thanks," Kelly murmured and unsuccessfully tried to disguise a wince. "In fact, I think I'll head for bed. I'll be fine in the morning, so don't worry about me."

But Jo Marie couldn't help doing just that. Little things about Kelly hadn't made sense in a long time— like staying home because of an argument with Mark. Kelly wasn't a shy, fledgling nurse. She'd stood her ground with Mark more than once. Even her behavior at the Christmas parties had been peculiar. Nor was Kelly a shrinking violet, yet she'd behaved like one. Obviously it was all an act. But her reasons remained unclear.

In the morning, Kelly announced that she was going to take a day of sick leave. Jo Marie studied her friend with worried eyes. Twice during the morning she phoned to see how Kelly was doing.

"Fine," Kelly answered impatiently the second time. "Listen, I'd probably be able to get some decent rest if I didn't have to get up and answer the phone every fifteen minutes."

In spite of her friend's testiness, Jo Marie chuckled. "I'll try to restrain myself for the rest of the day."

"That would be greatly appreciated."

"Do you want me to bring you something back for dinner?"

"No," she answered emphatically. "Food sounds awful."

Mark breezed into the office around noon, surprising Jo Marie. Sitting on the corner of her desk, he dangled one foot as she finished a telephone conversation.

"Business must be slow if you've got time to be dropping in here," she said, replacing the receiver.

"I come to take you to lunch and you're complaining?"

"You've come to ask about Kelly?" She wouldn't hedge. The time for playing games had long passed.

"Oh?" Briefly he arched a brow in question. "Is that so?"

"She's got the flu. There, I just saved you the price of lunch." Jo Marie couldn't disguise her irritation.

"You didn't save me the price of anything," Mark returned lazily. "I was going to let you treat."

Unable to remain angry with her brother for long, Jo Marie joined him in a nearby café a few minutes later, but neither of them mentioned Kelly again. By unspoken agreement, Kelly, Andrew, and Kelly's unexpected resignation were never mentioned.

Jo Marie's minestrone soup and turkey sandwich arrived and she unwrapped the silverware from the paper napkin. "How would you feel about a roommate for a while?" Jo Marie broached the subject tentatively.

"Male or female?" Dusky dark eyes so like her own twinkled with mischief.

"This may surprise you—female."

Mark laid his sandwich aside. "I'll admit my interest has been piqued."

"You may not be as keen once you find out that it's me."

"You?"

"Well I'm going to have to find someplace else to move sooner or later and—"

"And you're interested in the sooner," he interrupted.

"Yes." She wouldn't mention her reasons, but Mark was astute enough to figure it out for himself.

Peeling open his sandwich, Mark removed a thin slice of tomato and set it on the beige plate. "As long as you do the laundry, clean, and do all the cooking I won't object."

A smile hovered at the edges of her mouth. "Your generosity overwhelms me, brother dearest."

"Let me know when you're ready and I'll help you cart your things over."

"Thanks, Mark."

Briefly he looked up from his meal and grinned. "What are big brothers for?"

Andrew's car was in the apartment parking lot when Jo Marie stepped off the bus that evening after work. The darkening sky convinced her that waiting outside for him to leave would likely result in a drenching. Putting aside her fears, she squared her shoulders and tucked her hands deep within her pockets. When Kelly was home she usually didn't keep the door locked so Jo Marie was surprised to discover that it was. While digging through her purse, she was even more surprised to hear loud voices from the other side of the door.

"This has to stop," Andrew was arguing. "And soon."

"I know," Kelly cried softly. "And I agree. I don't want to ruin anyone's life."

"Three days."

"All right—just until Friday."

Jo Marie made unnecessary noise as she came through the door. "I'm home," she announced as she stepped into the living room. Kelly was dressed in her robe and slippers, slouched on the sofa. Andrew had apparently been pacing the carpet. She could feel his gaze seek her out. But she managed to avoid it, diverting her attention instead to the picture on the wall behind him. "If you'll excuse me I think I'll take a hot shower."

"Friday," Andrew repeated in a low, impatient tone.

"Thank you, Drew," Kelly murmured and sighed softly.

Kelly was in the same position on the sofa when Jo Marie returned, having showered and changed clothes. "How are you feeling?"

"Not good."

For Kelly to admit to as much meant that she'd had a miserable day. "Is there anything I can do?"

Limply, Kelly laid her head back against the back of the couch and closed her eyes. "No, I'm fine. But this is the worst case of stomach flu I can ever remember?"

"You're sure it's the flu?"

Slowly Kelly opened her eyes. "I'm the nurse here."

"Yes, your majesty." With a dramatic twist to her chin, Jo Marie bowed in mock servitude. "Now would you like me to fix you something for dinner?"

"No."

"How about something cool to drink?"

Kelly nodded, but her look wasn't enthusiastic. "Fine."

As the evening progressed, Jo Marie studied her friend carefully. It could be just a bad case of the stomach flu, but Jo Marie couldn't help but be concerned. Kelly had always been so healthy and full of life. When a long series of cramps doubled Kelly over in pain, Jo Marie reached for the phone.

"Mark, can you come over?" She tried to keep the urgency from her voice.

"What's up?"

"It's Kelly. She's sick." Jo Marie attempted to keep her voice low enough so her roommate wouldn't hear. "She keeps insisting it's the flu, but I don't know. She's in a lot of pain for a simple intestinal virus."

Mark didn't hesitate. "I'll be right there."

Ten minutes later he was at the door. He didn't bother to knock, letting himself in. "Where's the patient?"

"Jo Marie." Kelly's round eyes tossed her a look of burning resentment. "You called Mark?"

"Guilty as charged, but I wouldn't have if I didn't think it was necessary."

Tears blurred the blue gaze. "I wish you hadn't," she murmured dejectedly. "It's just the flu."

"Let me be the judge of that." Mark spoke in a crisp professional tone, kneeling at her side. He opened the small black bag and took out the stethoscope.

Not knowing what else to do, Jo Marie hovered at his side for instructions. "Should I boil water or something?"

"Call Drew," Kelly insisted. "He at least won't overreact to a simple case of the flu."

Mark's mouth went taut, but he didn't rise to the intended gibe.

Reluctantly Jo Marie did as she was asked. Andrew answered on the third ring. "Beaumont here."

"Andrew, this is—"

"Jo Marie," he finished for her, his voice carrying a soft rush of pleasure.

"Hi," she began awkwardly and bit into the corner of her bottom lip. "Mark's here. Kelly's not feeling well and I think she may have something serious. She wanted to know if you could come over."

"I'll be there in ten minutes." He didn't take a breath's hesitation.

As it was, he arrived in eight and probably set several speed records in the process. Jo Marie answered his hard knock. "What's wrong with Kelly? Sh seemed fine this afternoon." He directed his question to Mark.

"I'd like to take Kelly over to the hospital for a couple of tests."

Jo Marie noted the way her brother's jaw had tightened as if being in the same room with Andrew was a test of his endurance. Dislike exuded from every pore.

"No," Kelly protested emphatically. "It's just the stomach flu."

"With the amount of tenderness in the cecum?" Mark argued, shaking his head slowly from side to side in a mocking gesture.

"Mark's the doctor," Andrew inserted and Jo Marie could have kissed him for being the voice of reason in a room where little evidence of it existed.

"You think it's my appendix?" Kelly said with shocked disbelief.

"It isn't going to hurt to run a couple of tests," Mark countered, again avoiding answering a direct question.

"Why should you care?" Kelly's soft voice wavered uncontrollably. "After yesterday I would have thought..."

"After yesterday," Mark cut in sharply, "I realized that you were right and that I owe you an apology." His eyes looked directly into Kelly's and the softness Jo Marie had witnessed in his gaze at the hospital Christmas party returned. He reached for Kelly's hand, folding it in his own. "Will you accept my apology? What you said yesterday made a lot of sense, but at the time I was angry at the world and took it out on you. Forgive me?"

With a trembling smile, Kelly nodded. "Yes, of course I do."

The look they shared was both poignant and tender, causing Jo Marie to feel like an intruder. Briefly, she wondered what Andrew was thinking.

"If it does turn out that I need surgery would you be the one to do it for me?"

Immediately Mark lowered his gaze. "No."

His stark response was cutting and Kelly flinched. "There's no one else I'd trust as much as you."

"I said I wouldn't." Mark pulled the stethoscope from his neck and placed it inside his bag.

"Instead of fighting about it now, why don't we see what happens?" Jo Marie attempted to reason. "There's no need to argue."

"There's every reason," Andrw intervened. "Tell us, Mark, why wouldn't you be Kelly's surgeon if she needed one?"

Jo Marie stared at Andrew, her dark eyes filled with irritation. Backing Mark into a corner wouldn't help the situation. She wanted to step forward and defend her brother, but Andrew stopped her with an abrupt motion of his hand, apparently having read her intent.

"Who I chose as my patients is my business." Mark's tone was dipped in acid.

"Isn't Kelly one of your patients?" Andrew questioned calmly. "You did hurry over here when you heard she was sick."

Coming to a standing position, Mark ignored the question and the man. "Maybe you'd like to change clothes." He directed his comment to Kelly.

Shaking her head she said, "No, I'm not going anywhere."

"Those tests are important." Mark's control on his anger was a fragile thread. "You're going to the hospital."

Again, Kelly shook her head. "No, I'm not."

"You're being unreasonable." Standing with his feet braced apart, Mark looked as if he was willing to take her to the hospital by force if necessary.

"Why not make an agreement," Andrew suggested with cool-headed resolve. "Kelly will agree to the tests, if you agree to be her doctor."

Tiredly, Mark rubbed a hand over his jaw and chin. "I can't do that."

"Why not?" Kelly implored.

"Yes, Mark, why not?" Andrew taunted.

Her brother's mouth thinned grimly as he turned aside and clenched his fists. "Because it isn't good practice to work on the people you're involved with emotionally."

The corners of Kelly's mouth lifted in a sad smile. "We're not emotionally involved. You've gone out of your way to prove that to me. If you have any emotion for me it would be hate."

Mark's face went white and it looked for an instant as if Kelly had physically struck him. "Hate you?" he repeated incredulously. "Maybe," he replied in brutal honesty. "You're able to bring out every other emotion in me. I've taken out a lot of anger on you recently. Most of which you didn't deserve and I apologize for that." He paused and ran a hand through his hair, mussing it. "No, Kelly," he corrected, "I can't hate you. It would be impossible when I love you so much," he announced with an impassive expression and pivoted sharply.

A tense silence engulfed the room until Kelly let out a small cry. "You love me? All these months you've put me through this torment and you love me?" She threw back the blanket and stood, placing her hands defiantly on her hips.

"A lot of good it did me." Mark's angry gaze crossed the width of the room to hold hers. "You're engaged to Daddy Warbucks over there so what good would it do to let you know?"

Jo Marie couldn't believe what she was hearing and gave a nervous glance to Andrew. Casually standing to the side of the room, he didn't look the least disturbed by what was happening. If anything, his features were relaxed as if he were greatly relieved.

"And if you cared for me then why didn't you say something before now?" Kelly challenged.

Calmly he met her fiery gaze. "Because he's got money, you've got money. Tell me what can I offer you that could even come close to the things he can give you."

"And you relate love and happiness with things?" Her low words were scathing. "Let me tell you exactly what you can offer me, Mark Jubal Early. You have it in your power to give me the things that matter most in my life: your love, your friendship, your respect. And...and...if you turn around and walk out that door, by heaven I'll never forgive you."

"I have no intention of leaving," Mark snapped in return. "But I can't very well ask you to marry me when you're wearing another man's ring."

"Fine." Without hesitating Kelly slipped Andrew's diamond from her ring finger and handed it back to him. Lightly she brushed her mouth over his cheeks. "Thanks, Drew."

His hands cupped her shoulders as he kissed her back. "Much happiness, Kelly," he whispered.

Brother and sister observed the scene with open-mouthed astonishment.

Turning, Kelly moved to Mark's side. "Now," she breathed in happily, "if that was a proposal, I accept."

Mark was apprently too stunned to answer.

"Don't tell me you've already changed your mind?" Kelly muttered.

"No, I haven't changed my mind. What about the hospital tests?" he managed finally, his voice slightly raw as his eyes devoured her.

"Give me a minute to change." Kelly left the room and the three were left standing, Jo Marie and Mark staring blankly at each other. Everything was happening so fast that it was like a dream with dark shades of unreality.

Kelly reappeared and Mark tucked her arm in his. "We should be back in an hour," Mark murmured, but he only had eyes for the pert-faced woman on his arm. Kelly's gaze was filled with a happy radiance that brought tears of shared happiness to Jo Marie's eyes.

"Take your time and call if you need us," Andrew said as the happy couple walked toward the door.

Jo Marie doubted that either Kelly or Mark heard him. When she turned her attention to Andrew she discovered that he was already walking toward her. With eager strides he eliminated the distance separating them.

"As I recall, our agreement was that I wouldn't try to see you or contact you again while Kelly wore my engagement ring."

Her dark eyes smiled happily into his. "That's right."

"Then let's be rid of this thing once and for all." He led her into the kitchen where he carelessly tossed the diamond ring into the garbage.

Jo Marie gasped. Andrew was literally throwing away thousands of dollars. The diamond was the largest she had ever seen.

"The ring is as phony as the engagement."

Still unable to comprehend what he was saying, she shook her head to clear her thoughts. "What?"

"The engagement isn't any more real than that so-called diamond."

"Why?" Reason had escaped her completely.

His hands brought Jo Marie into the loving circle of his arms. "By Thanksgiving I'd given up every hope of ever finding you again. I'd convinced myself that those golden moments were just a figment of my imagination and that some quirk of fate had brought us together, only to pull us apart."

It seemed the most natural thing in the world to have his arms around her. Her eyes had filled with moisture so that his features swam in and out of her vision. "I'd given up hope of finding you, too," she admitted in an achingly soft voice. "But I couldn't stop thinking about you."

Tenderly he kissed her, briefly tasting the sweetness of her lips. As if it was difficult to stop, he drew in an uneven breath and rubbed his jaw over the top of her head, mussing her hair. "I saw Kelly at her parents' house over the Thanksgiving holiday and she was miserable. We've always been close for second cousins and we had a long talk. She told me that she'd been in love with Mark for months. The worst part was that she was convinced that he shared her feelings, but his pride was holding him back. Apparently your brother has some strange ideas about wealth and position.''

''He's learning,'' Jo Marie murmured, still caught in the rapture of being in Andrew's arms. ''Give him time.'' She said this knowing that Kelly was willing to devote the rest of her life to Mark.

''I told Kelly she should give him a little competition and if someone showed an interested in her, then Mark would step forward. But apparently she'd already tried that.''

''My brother can be as stubborn as ten men.''

''I'm afraid I walked into this phony engagement with my eyes wide open. I said that if Mark was worth his salt, he wouldn't stand by and let her marry another man. If he loved her, really loved her, he'd step in.''

''But he nearly didn't.''

''No,'' Andrew admitted. ''I was wrong. Mark loved Kelly enough to sacrifice his own desires to give her what he thought she needed. I realized that the night of my Christmas party. By that time I was getting desperate. I'd found you and every minute of this engagement was agony. In desperation, I tried to talk to Mark. But that didn't work. He assumed I was warning him off Kelly and told me to make her happy or I'd pay the consequences.''

The irony of the situation was almost comical. ''You were already suffering the consequences. Why didn't you say something? Why didn't you explain?''

''Oh, love, if you'd been anyone but Mark's sister I would have.'' Again his mouth sought hers as if he couldn't get enough of her kisses. ''Here I was trapped in the worst set of circumstances I've ever imagined. The woman who had haunted me for months was within my grasp and I was caught in a steel web."

"I love you, Andrew. I've loved you from the moment you held me all those months ago. I knew then that you were meant to be someone special in my life."

"This has taught me the most valuable lesson of my life." He arched her close. So close it was impossible to breath normally. "I'll never let you out of my arms again. I'm yours for life, Jo Marie, whether you want me or not. I've had to trust again every instinct that you would wait for me. Dear Lord, I had visions of you falling in love with Jim Rowden, and the worst part was I couldn't blame you if you did. I can only imagine what kind of man you thought me."

Lovingly, Jo Marie spread kisses over his face. "It's going to take me a lifetime to tell you."

"Oh, love." His grip tightened against the back of her waist, arching her closer until it was almost painful to breathe. Not that Jo Marie cared. Andrew was holding her and had promised never to let her go again.

"I knew something was wrong with you and Kelly from the beginning," she murmured between soft, exploring kisses. Jo Marie couldn't have helped but notice.

"I've learned so much from this," Andrew confessed. "I think I was going slowly mad. I want more than to share my life with you, Jo Marie. I want to see our children in your arms. I want to grow old with you at my side."

"Oh, Andrew." Her arms locked around his neck and the tears of happiness streamed down her face.

"I love you, Florence Nightingale."

"And you, Andrew Beaumont, will always be my dream man."

"Forever?" His look was skeptical.

She lifted her mouth to his. "For all eternity," she whispered in promise.

"An ulcer?" Jo Marie shook her head slowly.

"Well, with all the stress I was under in the past few weeks, it's little wonder," Kelly defended herself.

The four sat in the living room sipping hot cocoa. Kelly was obediently drinking plain heated milk and hating it. But her eyes were warm and happy as they rested on Mark who was beside her with an arm draped over her shoulders.

"I've felt terrible about all this, Jo Marie," Kelly continued. "Guilt is a horrible companion. I didn't know exactly what was going on with you and Andrew. But he let it be known that he was in love with you and wanted this masquerade over quickly."

"You felt guilty?" Mark snorted. "How do you think I felt kissing another man's fiancée?"

"About the same way Jo Marie and I felt," Andrew returned with a chuckle.

"You know, Beaumont. Now that you're marrying my sister, I don't think you're such a bad character after all."

"That's encouraging."

"I certainly hope you get along since you're both going to be standing at the altar at the same time."

Three pairs of blank eyes stared at Kelly. "Double wedding, silly. It makes sense, doesn't it? The four of us have been through a lot together. It's only fitting we start our new lives at the same time."

"But soon," Mark said emphatically. "Sometime in January."

Everything was moving so fast, Jo Marie barely had time to assimilate the fact that Andrew loved her and she was going to share his life.

"Why not?" she agreed with a small laugh. "We've yet to do anything else conventionally."

Her eyes met Andrew's. They'd come a long way, all four of them, but they'd stuck it out through the doubts and the hurts. Now their whole lives stretched before them filled with promise.

READERS' COMMENTS ON SILHOUETTE ROMANCES:

"The best time of my day is when I put my children to bed at naptime and sit down to read a Silhouette Romance. Keep up the good work."

P.M.*, Allegan, MI

"I am very fond of the quality of your Silhouette Romances. They are so real. I have tried to read some of the other romances, but I always come back to Silhouette."

C.S., Mechanicsburg, PA

"I feel that Silhouette Books offer a wider choice and/or variety than any of the other romance books available."

R.R., Aberdeen, WA

"I have enjoyed reading Silhouette Romances for many years now. They are light and refreshing. You can always put yourself in the main characters' place, feeling alive and beautiful."

J.M.K., San Antonio, TX

"My boyfriend always teases me about Silhouette Books. He asks me, how's my love life and naturally I say terrific, but I tell him that there is always room for a little more romance from Silhouette."

F.N., Ontario, Canada

*names available on request

Take 4
Silhouette Special Edition novels
FREE...

and preview
future
books
in your
home for
15 days!

Start with 4 FREE books, yours to keep. Then
preview 6 brand-new Special Edition® novels—
delivered right to your door every month—as soon
as they are published.

When you decide to keep them, pay just $1.9
each ($2.50 each in Canada), *with no shipping
handling, or other additional charges of an
kind!*

Romance *is* alive, well and flourishing in th
moving love stories presented by Silhouette Speci
Edition. They'll awaken your desires, enliven yo
senses, and leave you tingling all over with excit
ment. In each romance-filled story you'll live ar
breathe the emotions of love and the satisfaction
romance triumphant.

You won't want to miss a single one of the heart-felt stories presented by Silhouette Special Edition; and when you take advantage of this special offer, you won't have to.

You'll also receive a FREE subscription to the Silhouette Books Newsletter as long as you remain a member. Each lively issue is filled with news on upcoming titles, interviews with your favorite authors, even their favorite recipes.

To become a home subscriber and receive your first 4 books FREE, fill out and mail the coupon today!

Silhouette Special Edition®

Silhouette Books, 120 Brighton Rd., P.O. Box 5084, Clifton, NJ 07015-5084

Clip and mail to: Silhouette Books,
120 Brighton Road, P.O. Box 5084,
Clifton, NJ 07015-5084*

YES. Please send me 4 FREE Silhouette Special Edition novels. Unless you hear from me after I receive them, send me 6 new Silhouette Special Edition novels to preview each month. I understand you will bill me just $1.95 each, a total of $11.70 (in Canada, $2.50 each, a total of $15.00), with no shipping, handling, or other charges of any kind. There is no minimum number of books that I must buy, and I can cancel at any time. The first 4 books are mine to keep.   **BS28R6**

Name _____ (please print)

Address _____ Apt. #

City _____ State/Prov. _____ Zip/Postal Code

* In Canada, mail to: Silhouette Canadian Book Club, 320 Steelcase Rd., E., Markham, Ontario, L3R 2M1, Canada
Terms and prices subject to change.
SILHOUETTE SPECIAL EDITION is a service mark and registered trademark.   SE-SUB-2

COMING NEXT MONTH

AFTER THE MUSIC—Diana Palmer
Rock singer Sabina Cane had been warned that Hamilton Thorndon was a formidable man, but nothing could have prepared her for the impact he would have on her life.

FAMILY SECRETS—Ruth Langan
Who was blackmailing Trudy St. Martin? Caine St. Martin and Ivy Murdock joined forces to discover the culprit's identity, and in the process they discovered the secrets of love.

THE HIGHEST TOWER—Ann Hurley
BeeGee was fearless enough to join the Greenings in their work as steeplejacks, but when her heart started falling for Dan Greening she became determined to keep her feet firmly on the ground.

HEART SHIFT—Glenda Sands
Arson...someone had burned down Chris's shop. Chris felt lucky that handsome and imposing Ian West was on the case, until he told her that she was the prime suspect.

THE CATNIP MAN—Barbara Turner
Julia treated life as a serious matter until, aboard a Mississippi riverboat, she met Chad. His infectious good nature chipped away at her reserve and brought laughter and love to her heart.

MINE BY WRITE—Marie Nicole
Professor Kyle McDaniels gladly offered to help Mindy Callaghan with her writing, yet when it came to offering his heart, he was the one who needed a little help.